Rise of the Wolf:
Katalya's Story

A Gateway Universe Novella

I0688948

Brian Dorsey

Glossary

The following glossary is provided for those unfamiliar with the Gateway novel series. More information on the series and the Gateway Universe in general is available at www.mountaineerwest.com

Alpha Humana: The most remote planet in the vast Xennite Empire.

Elite Guard: Alpha Humana's most elite military unit. Since the Peace Accords, the Elite Guard has carried out a clandestine war against the Terillian Scout Rangers in the Neutral Quadrant (commonly called the Dark Zone), the Demilitarized Zone between the Xen Empire and the Terillian Confederation.

First Families: Ruling elite of Alpha Humana. One hundred fifty families control all land on the planet and select representatives to the Senate which serves as the ruling body under control of the ProConsul.

Gateway Station: Communications station on the Humani side of the Neutral Quadrant. It controls a vast series of satellites and smaller stations that act as an early warning system if the Terillian's were to enter Xen space.

Neutral Quadrant: Also known in common language as the Dark Zone. Many of the planets in this quadrant were devastated by the long war and with the signing of the Peace Accords, the rest fell into decay. Their original names replaced with alpha-numeric identifiers during the Accords, dozens of habitable worlds fell under control of warlords, tyrants, and mercenaries. Others still try to scrape out an existence while at the same time defend themselves from raiders, slaver traders, and would-be rulers in the now isolated section of the galaxy between the two superpowers. Although no large military operations are authorized as part of the Accords, both the Xen (through the Humani Elite Guard) and the Terillian Scout Rangers have carried out a clandestine war against each other for generations with the Dark Zone.

Peace Accords: Cease fire signed by the Xen Empire and the Terillian Confederation over 150 years ago. It created the Neutral Quadrant.

Praetorians: The ProConsul's personal military unit.

Scout Rangers: The Terillian Confederations most elite unit and sworn enemies of the Humani Elite Guard.

Terillian Confederation: Historical enemies of the Xennite Empire, particularly the Humani civilization.

Xennite Empire: An alliance of three civilizations under the rule of the Xen Emperor. These civilizations are the Xen, the Dorans, and the Humani.

Chapter 1

Katalya Skye, her raven hair dripping with oil, fumed as she chased her sister down the passageway of the research ship, *Mendeleev.*

"Get back here, you brat!" she yelled, watching Mori dart into their father's research lab.

When she turned the corner, she saw Mori standing behind her father, Renard, with a guilty smile painted on her face and gloating laughter in her brilliant green eyes.

"Don't hide behind father, Ino'ka," fumed Katalya, using her sister's Akota name.

"It's not my fault you didn't move, Kimimila" replied Mori, taunting her sister.

Mori, eight years old and four years younger than her sister, was a troublemaker and everyone on the *Mendeleev* knew it. Because both of her parents had dreamt she would become a warrior, she was allowed to run wild just like an Akota boy. She'd even started wearing her hair in the three-weave braids worn by the elite Ki'etsenko warriors.

"You two stop it," ordered Renard, pulling Katalya in close. He knelt so he could look into her eyes. "And stop using your Akota names in the lab … you know there are non-Akota here. You both know better," he added with a stern look toward Mori.

"Yes, ahte … Father," replied Katalya, correcting herself.

"Yes, Father," added Mori.

"Now what is the problem?" asked Renard.

"She dropped a whole bucket of oil on me," grumbled Katalya, "and I was just getting ready to go study with Cain Two-Rivers."

"It wasn't my fault," pleaded Mori. "I was just trying to see how much oil was in a hydraulic lift … I was going to put it back … and she walked under the platform when I knocked it off. It wasn't my fault … it was the artificial gravity."

Katalya looked up toward her father. "Father?" she huffed.

"And besides," added Mori, "she wasn't going to study with Cain. She was gonna just stare into his eyes and think about kissing him … yuck."

"Mori!" shouted Katalya. She knew her face had to be at least two shades darker than her normal olive. "Father, we were gonna study, I promise."

"You two need to stop fighting," said Renard. "How many times have your mother and I spoke to you about the importance of family and the clan?"

Katalya clinched her teeth. "Yes, Father, but she —"

"Enough!" interrupted Renard. "You two hug each other."

"Father!" groaned Mori. "She's covered in oil."

"That you put there, Mori," added Renard. "Which means you will clean up the mess you made and do your sister's chores for the next two days."

Katalya couldn't hold back her smile. It wasn't often Mori was called on her games.

"Fine," replied Mori, her arms wrapped tightly around her torso.

"Now is that the behavior expected of a leader?" Renard asked Mori.

Mori slowly let her arms fall to her side. "No," she said softly. "And I should have been more careful." She looked up toward Katalya, opening her arms. "Sorry."

Katalya stepped into Mori's embrace. She was already so strong, Katalya thought as her sister squeezed tightly. "It's okay," she added.

"See," said Renard, "all you needed to —"

The blasting of the ships alarm and the flashing of the emergency lights interrupted Renard, causing Katalya to jump.

"ALL SECURITY PERSONNEL TO STATIONS, ALL CIVILIANS AND CONTRACTORS STAND FAST. SHUT ALL AIR LOCKS AND SECURITY DOORS."

"What is happening?" asked Mori.

"I don't know," he replied. "But we need to stay here."

"Renard!" shouted Katalya's mother, bursting through the door. "It's slavers!"

"This far out?" replied Renard, his face red and tight. "Aren't we supposed to have a military escort?"

"I heard one of the crewmembers say the slavers have more than one ship … they took out our escort," huffed Katalya's mother.

Katalya's heart raced as she grabbed her mother's arm tightly. She felt Mori's arm around her waist and looked down toward her.

"Don't worry, cu'we. I'll protect you," said Mori with a smile, although Katalya could tell she was scared too.

"INTRUDER ALERT! INTURDER ALERT! SECURITY TEAM TO THE STARBOARD STORAGE BAY."

"They've boarded us!" shouted Katalya's mother.

"Sierra, hide the children," ordered Renard, grabbing a metal bar used to pry open stuck airlocks from the wall.

"Can we try to get to an escape pod?"

"They would just scoop us up as we floated along," replied Renard. "We have a better chance staying onboard.

"Are they going to take us?" Katalya asked her mother.

"No, little one," replied Sierra. "Our security teams will stop them, but we need to hide and stay out of the way."

Katalya saw her mother look toward her father, her eyes screaming with anxiety.

"Over there … the cabinets," said Renard.

"Let's go girls," replied Sierra, leading Katalya and Mori to a set of vented cabinets in a corner of the lab.

Katalya read the labels on the doors: DANGER: RADIOACTIVE. She looked up toward Sierra. "Mother?"

Sierra read the sign and glanced toward Renard.

"It's okay," shouted Katalya's father. "They would have to stay in there for days for it to hurt them. But the slavers don't know that."

"Let's go," said Sierra, turning back toward her daughters and opening the first door. "Mori, you get in here and don't come out until it's safe."

"Yes, Mother," replied Mori as she climbed into the cabinet.

Katalya had already opened the cabinet across from Mori when her mother turned toward her. "We'll be okay, Mother," she said. "What are you going to do?"

Katalya felt her mother's hand on her cheek.

"We're gonna fight, baby," she replied, tears running down her cheek. "You just stay put. No matter what."

"Yes, Mother," said Katalya, her voice cracking.

"Stay," added her mother as she pushed the cabinet door closed.

Katalya's body trembled as she huddled inside the cabinet, the sound of her breathing filling the small space.

Her body jerked at the sound of gunfire in the hallway outside of the lab and Katalya placed her hands over her mouth.

"Don't come out, girls," she heard her mother shout.

Katalya closed her eyes, her body shaking. Her body tensed and she let out a muffled shriek as the sound of the door being kicked open shot through the lab. She opened her eyes to see her father sliding across the floor as she peered through the tiny vents in the cabinet door.

Katalya heard her mother scream as she saw a slaver slam her father back onto the floor with his boot. Her gaze was fixed on her father as he struggled against the weight of the slaver standing over him. He glanced toward her hiding spot.

"No!" Katalya heard her mother shout as she saw the slaver point a pistol toward her father's head.

The pistol cracked as Renard's head bounced and fell back onto the floor, blood instantly pooling around him.

Unable to control herself, Katalya let out a scream.

The man standing over the body of her father spun toward the cabinet. "What was that?" he said.

"There's someone hiding in there," came another voice. "Open it up."

"It's radioactive," replied the man with pistol.

"Just open it and grab whoever's inside … just be quick."

"No," Katalya heard her mother plead only to be cut short by the sound a powerful hand landing on her jaw.

"Shut up, bitch," she heard someone say.

Her heart raced and her body trembled as the man with the pistol walked closer and closer.

The door flew open and a large bearded man peered into the cabinet. "Looky here," he said with a smile. Katalya kicked at him frantically as he grabbed her arm and threw her onto the floor.

She hit the ground next to her father's lifeless body. She wrapped her arms around his body, wailing.

"Come here," said the man, lifting her body into the air.

"Leave her alone!" shouted her mother.

Katalya, still struggling against the man holding her, looked up to see her mother. Two slavers stood over her, holding her on her knees a few meters away. One of the men reached down and slapped her across the face again. "I told you to shut up!" he ordered.

A fourth slaver put his hand to his ear to listen to a report on his communications device. "Ship's secure," he reported.

"We got time for some fun?" asked one of the men standing above Sierra.

"Why not," answered the man with the communication device. "Just don't mess them up too much for tradin' when you're done," he added before exiting the lab.

"Nice," replied the man holding Katalya, throwing her onto a nearby table.

The air left her lungs as her back slammed against the hard surface. Test tubes and lab equipment shattered as she struggled in vain.

Gasping for breath, her nose burned as the chemicals on the table began to release a noxious odor. The sensation in her nose disappeared when she felt the rough hand of the slaver running down the outside of her leg. Her body went stiff and her eyes shot toward her mother. The sandpaper feel of his touch traced back up to her thigh and she closed her eyes.

"No," pleaded Sierra. "Not her ... just ... just ... I'll do anything."

Katalya felt the man remove his hand from her inner thigh and she opened her eyes.

"But this one would be so sweet," he said, running a hand over her cheek.

"Please," said Sierra, now pulled to her feet by the two men. "You want a woman, not a child," she continued as she let her dress fall to the ground.

"Maybe so," said the man, shoving Katalya off the table. "Come over here," he ordered.

Katalya hit the floor and scooted back against the wall, trembling in fear. She glanced toward the cabinet where Mori was hiding, wanting so badly to crawl inside with her.

"You better make this worth it, Terillian bitch," said the man as Sierra walked over to him. "And not just for me," he added as two other men grabbed her and pushed her over the table.

"Close your eyes, Katalya," shouted Sierra.

Katalya obeyed, closing her eyes, pulling her knees to her chest, and turning her head toward the floor. Staring at the floor, she saw her father's blood start to trickle under her feet as she tried to block out the laughter of the slavers and the cries of her mother.

***

"Damn," said the last of the slavers, pushing Sierra's naked body onto the floor.

"We'd better get these two on the ship," said another.

"Yes," replied the bearded man. "Get dressed, Terillian trash," he added, tossing Sierra her dress.

Katalya felt her head pulled upward as the man grabbed her hair and yanked it toward the overhead.

Her tear-filled eyes met his.

The man leaned in close. Katalya could smell the musty odor of his sweaty body. She tried to turn her head away from him, but he wouldn't let her.

"Your mother must really love you," said the man with a smile.

Katalya glanced over to her mother who was pulling her dress back over her body. Their eyes met, but Sierra, her hair matted and face red, turned away.

Her view of her mother was blocked when the bearded man leaned in close to her face again. "But don't worry my little peach, I'm still gonna get a taste."

The man jerked Katalya to her feet and began to drag her away. Katalya looked back toward the cabinet where Mori was hiding.

Chapter 2

Katalya squeezed her mother tightly as they sat in the cold cell of the slaver's ship, her body still shaking.

"It will be okay, Katalya," her mother said, running her hand over Katalya's hair, still coated in oil.

She looked up toward her mother. Her face was tight and her eyes held a vacant stare. Katalya knew her mother didn't believe her own words.

"There's my two little birds," came a voice from outside of the cell.

Katalya looked up to see the bearded man. His eyes slowly looked up and down her body, making her stomach turn.

"I told you I was gonna get a taste, little bird," continued the man, unlocking the door.

"No," said Sierra, stepping in front of Katalya. "Take me."

"Already been there," replied the man. "Even though you were sweet, this one's got to be so much sweeter."

"She's just a child," pleaded Sierra.

"I'll be the judge of that," replied the man as he opened the door.

Katalya wrapped her arms around her mother's waist and closed her eyes when she felt his hand touch her shoulder.

"What are you doing, Tamar?" asked a tall, muscular man who had just entered the room.

"Nothing, Captain," replied Tamar. "Just gonna —"

"I know what you were just gonna do," replied the slave ship captain. "I told you assholes to leave the young ones alone. We'll get twice as much if they're pure."

"But I was just gonna play a little," replied Tamar.

"Are you gonna pay the 5000 credits I'll lose if you ruin her?"

Tamar paused. "You're lucky, little bird," he said with a scowl to Katalya as he turned toward Sierra. "But you," he added, grabbing Sierra's arm. "We're gonna go for a little walk."

Tamar pulled Sierra in close and ran his tongue over her neck as Sierra stared blankly at the overhead. "Let's go," said Tamar, pulling Sierra toward the cell door.

"Leave her alone!" shouted Katalya, grabbing Tamar's arm.

A boot from Tamar sent Katalya flying backwards across the cell, but she quickly pushed herself to her feet and started at him again.

"Stop!" ordered Sierra.

Katalya saw the stern look on her mother's face. "Remember, do as you are told and keep your mind and heart separate from your body."

"Better listen to your mama, little one," smiled Tamar. "And just be glad you ain't goin' for any walks yet."

***

The sound of the cell door opening jarred Katalya out of her exhausted sleep. She looked up to see her mother pushed back into the cell.

"You're gonna make someone a lot of money in a rec house," said Tamar, a satisfied smile painted on his face. "Maybe even as much as the little one."

Katalya looked toward her mother as she lay on the floor of the cell. Her lip was swollen and bleeding.

"I'm gonna kill you," said Katalya rushing toward Tamar.

As she reached the slaver, Tamar shoved her onto the ground with a laugh. "You are full of fire … it's really a shame," he added, stepping outside of the cell and locking the door.

Katalya turned and rushed toward her mother. Kneeling next to her, she put her arms around her torso.

Sierra winced when Katalya's hand touched her ribs.

"Are you okay, mother?"

"I'm fine, Katalya," replied Sierra with a forced smile. "He can't hurt my heart or my mind."

Katalya's heart ached for her mother and her body shook thinking that this would also be her fate. "Won't someone come for us?"

"No," replied Sierra with a bluntness that hit Katalya like a hammer. "We must prepare to survive on our own, Katalya."

"What about Mori?"

"She'll be okay," replied Sierra. She paused. Katalya felt her mother's hands on her cheeks. "You must listen to what I'm going to tell you," she continued as tears welled up in her eyes. "You must stay alive, Katalya."

"I —"

"Listen," interrupted Sierra. "They may take you away from me and you will be on your own."

"No, Mother —"

"It will happen, baby, and I won't be able to stop them so you must do what I say."

"Yes," replied Katalya, gripping her mother's arm with all of her strength.

"The Great Spirit has more in store for you; I know it," Sierra continued. "But it will not be easy. You must use your head to survive while staying Akota in your heart."

"I don't understand."

"I won't be able to protect you and ..." Sierra paused, closing her eyes and taking a heavy breath. "... and things will happen to you that will hurt both your body and your spirit, but you must separate what is happening to you from who you are, my daughter. No matter what happens to your body you must not let it get to here or here," she said, placing her finger on Katalya's forehead and then chest over her heart. "Let your mind take you to a place that is happy and let your heart always remind you of your family and your clan."

"What about you, Mother?" asked Katalya, tears rolling down her cheeks.

"I will stay with you as long as I can, Katalya. After that, remember that I love you with all of my heart."

"I will," replied Katalya.

Sierra placed her hands on Katalya's cheeks again, forcing her to look directly into her red, swollen eyes. "When it gets bad, let your heart allow your mind to drift away from your body. Once you learn to leave your body you must do as you are told and whatever you need to in order to survive." Desperation covered Sierra's face as she continued. "But when the chance to run comes ..."

Katalya felt her mother's hands tighten.

"... you run," she said through clenched teeth.

Chapter 3

"What's happening Mother?" asked Katalya as she watched the slavers move back and forth in the cargo bay. The last two weeks had been a nightmare of taunts and threats punctuated by daily visits as Tamar took her mother for their walks. A few times he hadn't even bothered leaving the cell. On those occasions, Katalya had curled herself into a ball in the corner of the cell, closing her eyes and covering her ears.

But now there seemed to be much more activity as slavers moved about grabbing equipment and gear.

"We've landed," replied Sierra, placing her hands on the bars of the cell and looking from side to side.

As they watched, Tamar stopped in front of the cell. Sierra took a step away from the bars, but Tamar grabbed her and pulled her as close to him as was possible through the bars.

"I'm gonna miss our little walks," he said, running his hand over her body. "But I guess it's time to get paid." He looked down toward Katalya. "And you're gonna bring a pretty penny, girly," he added before turning his attention back to her mother. "And you … you're gonna be so popular," he said, leaning in close. "You're gonna be ridden by so many miners and slavers that you'll think back to our walks and wish it was this good."

With one last lecherous glance, Tamar turned and walked away.

"Mother?" Katalya's heart pounded. This is the day her mother had been warning her about. She saw desperation and anxiety painted over her mother's face.

"Quickly, get the spoon from the bowl."

Katalya didn't understand but complied and grabbed the spoon from a bowl of stew they had been given earlier.

"Here, Mother."

Sierra grabbed the spoon and began rubbing it against the metal of the bars as fast as she could.

"What are you doing?"

"Trying to make it sharp," replied Sierra as she rapidly raked the handle of the spoon back and forth across the bars.

"Are we going to fight?"

"No, baby," replied Sierra. "If we fight, they will kill us."

"Then why are you doing this?"

Sierra stopped and examined the rough, jagged edge of the spoon.

"Mother?"

"Katalya," replied Sierra. "Kneel down."

"But —"

"Just do it," ordered Sierra.

Katalya slowly knelt on the cold, hard floor as her mother did the same.

"It's time you let your mind wonder," said Sierra.

"What are you going to do?" begged Katalya as Sierra held the sharp, ragged spoon handle to her head.

"I'm trying to keep you as safe as I can," replied Sierra, grabbing Katalya's hair.

Katalya clenched her jaw and grunted as her mother pulled her hair hard and started slicing through it with the jagged spoon handle.

"Ouch," said Katalya as the spoon pulled against the roots of her hair.

"You can't look pretty when they take us to the market," declared Sierra, continuing to pull and slice at Katalya's long hair.

Katalya closed her eyes and gritted her teeth as her mother cut and yanked on her hair.

"There," declared Sierra after a few painful moments.

Katalya opened her eyes to see clumps and strands of hair all around her on the floor.

"You're so beautiful," said Sierra, cupping Katalya's head as tears raced down her face. "Too beautiful," she added closing her eyes. She paused. "I love you, baby … you know that, right?"

"Yes, Mother," replied Katalya. "I —"

Katalya was cut short as Sierra punched her in the jaw, knocking her backwards onto the floor.

"Why?" cried Katalya as she grabbed for her cheek, pain radiating across her face.

"If you look pretty," said Sierra, her face red and soaked with tears, "you will be sold and men like Tamar will —"

Katalya let out a groan as her mother grabbed her again and pulled off the floor only to land another blow to the side of her face. Hitting the floor again, Katalya pulled her knees to her chest and wept.

"Let me see you," said Sierra.

Katalya felt her mother pull her off the floor again and prepared for another blow.

"That should do it," said Sierra, pulling Katalya into an embrace.

Katalya leaned against her mother, whimpering as Sierra rocked her back and forth.

"I love you so much, baby," cried Sierra.

"I know," huffed Katalya, beginning to sob. "I don't want to leave you."

"I know, honey. I don't want to leave you either," added Sierra as she placed her hand on the back of Katalya's head and directed her to look into her mother's eyes.

"But I will always be with you ... and so will your father and Mori.

Katalya felt her mother's hand on her chest.

"In here, your family and clan will live forever so if you stay alive, so do we."

"Yes, Mother," replied Katalya.

"What the fuck is going on here?" Katalya heard a man shout.

She turned to see the ship's captain at the cell door.

"You, girl ... stand up!" he ordered.

Katalya stood and looked toward the man, her left eye partially shut from the swelling.

"What the ... you ... Tamar!" shouted the captain. "Get your ass over here."

"What is it?" replied Tamar, walking toward the cell.

"What the fuck did you do to this girl?"

"Damn ... I didn't do that. You told me to leave her alone."

"Then who the ..." The captain paused. "Her mother."

"What?" asked Tamar.

"That Terillian bitch cut her hair and beat her up so we couldn't sell her to a recreation house right away."

The captain, his face red with rage, opened the door and stepped inside. As he walked toward Katalya, she stepped backwards. "Stop!" he ordered as he snagged her arm and pulled her toward him. He grabbed her jaw and twisted her head from right to left. "Fucking ruined!" he cursed, shoving her onto the ground.

Katalya looked up as the captain turned toward her mother.

"And you," he said, slapping Sierra across the face with all of his strength.

Sierra's head snapped to the right from the blow, but she turned back toward him defiantly.

"Fine, Terillian whore. Have it your way." The captain turned toward two other slavers standing at the door. "Get whatever you can from whoever you can for the little one and this one," he said, locking his gaze on Sierra. "Sell her to the dirtiest rec house you can find."

Chapter 4

Katalya clung to her mother's arm as the two were shuffled off the ship.

She closed her eyes against the brightness of the day. Her vision adjusting, Katalya saw dozens of people walking about the crowded market.

She saw an old cook chopping up the shoulder meat of some large animal at his food stand. To her right, a middle-aged lady haggled with a fat merchant over the price of a leather bag. Two miners walked past, turning their heads to gaze at her mother.

All around them, people were going about their daily lives while Katalya's was about to be ripped apart.

"Keep moving," grunted Tamar, giving Katalya a shove.

Stumbling forward, Katalya regained her balance but was stopped by a man grabbing her arm. She looked up to see a well-dressed man with deep blue eyes and salt and pepper hair. "What did you do to this one?" he asked.

"Wasn't us," replied the captain of the slaver ship. "Crazy bitch of a mother did this to her when we landed."

"Hmm," replied the man calmly before grabbing Sierra and pulling her close to him.

Katalya jumped, startled from the powerful open hand the man landed across Sierra's cheek. The sound of the slap echoed through Katalya's mind like a gunshot as her mother stumbled from the force of the blow. Regaining her footing, Sierra stared defiantly at the man.

"Smart one, aren't you?" said the man. "But it will only delay the inevitable." He turned toward the slavers. "Didn't I tell you to separate the mothers and daughters?"

Tamar and the ship's captain glanced at each other and looked back toward the man.

"Never mind," continued the man. "Take the little one to the labor market and this one …" He paused looking over Sierra. "… take her to the recreation market."

"Mother!" shouted Katalya as Tamar ripped her away from her mother's embrace.

"Be strong!" yelled Sierra, tears flowing down her face. "Remember what I told you …"

Katalya saw the desperation in her eyes. "Survive!" she shouted. "Survive."

Katalya kicked and twisted her body as Tamar dragged her away. "No! No!" she wailed as her mother faded into the crowd.

As she lost sight of her mother, panic erupted from every fiber of Katalya's soul as she flailed against Tamar's hold.

Suddenly, her vision blurred and pain exploded in her head as Tamar slammed his fist into her jaw.

"Shut up!" he ordered, pulling her limp body into the air. "You're already bruised so if you don't stop, I'll smack you around some more," he added, the stench of his alcohol-soaked breath bringing Katalya back to full consciousness.

"I won't fight," conceded Katalya, remembering her mother's words.

"Good," replied Tamar, lowering her to the ground. "'Bout time you learned some damn manners ... or maybe you just need to be smacked around a little first."

Hatred and fear pumped through her body like fire, making her nauseous as Tamar walked her to a large brick building. Above the entrance was a large sign flashing the Terillian symbols for 'servant' and 'sales' as well as those of other languages she didn't understand.

Tamar pounded on the door and a small, round man in a tan shirt and black pants opened swung it open. He fiddled with an electronic ledger as two security guards stood behind him.

"For sale?" asked the man with the ledger.

"Yes," replied Tamar.

"Any minimum limits?"

"No."

"Very well," replied the man. "Shall I see your factor's code?"

"Here," said Tamar, extending a chip for the man to scan.

"Very well," replied the man after scanning the chip. "Let's see … her?"

Katalya shuffled forward, helped with a nudge from Tamar. She tensed as one of the guards grabbed her arm, extending it outward.

A small prick caused her to grimace as the man injected something into her right arm.

"What is that?" she asked.

"Just a little tracker so your old owner gets paid and your new one can find you if you try to run," replied the man with a smile. "There we go," he added, running a scanner over her arm and checking the readout. He looked toward Tamar. "The exchange is complete. Tell your factor that the purchase price, minus the standard house handling fee, will be sent to their credit repository within one standard hour of sale."

"Whatever," replied Tamar, kneeling down to look directly into Katalya's eyes.

She tried to turn away, but he grabbed her jaw with a powerful, dirty hand and forced her to face him.

"Maybe I'll come back in a few years and look you up," he said through stained teeth. "That way I can give you some of what I gave your mother."

"I must ask you to let the girl go," interrupted the man with the ledger. "We must get her prepared."

"Fine," grunted Tamar. He leaned in close, sniffing around Katalya's neck.

Katalya closed her eyes in disgust.

"Don't forget about me little girly," he said with grin. "'Cause I won't forget about you," he added, running his tongue over her neck before standing and walking away.

Katalya stood motionless with her eyes closed, unable to comprehend her new reality.

"Okay, girl," said the man with the ledger. "Follow the guard."

"Why?" asked Katalya.

"The sooner you stop asking why, little one, the easier your new life will be," he replied. "Now follow the guard."

Katalya turned and followed the guard to into a small room. Inside the cramped room, four older women were undressing, cleaning, and dressing four young girls. She stepped inside and the door closed behind her, causing her to turn toward the noise.

"Come on," came a voice from behind her as Katalya felt her body being abruptly turned away from the door. "Quickly," continued the old woman in front of her, removing Katalya's shoes. Next, the woman began to pull Katalya's shirt over her head. She resisted but a light rap on her wrist from the woman stopped her resistance.

"Don't fuss," said the woman, yanking the shirt over Katalya's raised arms. "Now the pants."

Katalya stared blankly at the woman, who returned a scowl.

"Hurry," she ordered, tugging at Katalya's waistline. "We need to get you cleaned up."

Katalya closed her eyes, pushed her pants to the floor, and stepped out of them.

"Oh," declared the woman. "You're pretty … and starting to grow." The woman leaned in close. "You're lucky you ended up here instead of the recreation auction," she continued, gripping Katalya's arms. "You keep your body covered and your hair short as long as you can."

Katalya felt the woman's hand on her cheek.

"Now move on to the next station."

Katalya, covered in goosebumps and shivering from the cold air, moved to the next woman in line.

"Hands up," directed the woman at the second station.

Katalya saw a large scar running the length of the woman's wrinkled face.

"Hands up!"

Katalya felt pressure under her arms and lifted them into the air.

The splash of warm water contrasted the cold air of the room and she looked toward the ceiling as the woman vigorously scrubbed Katalya's body.

"What's this?" asked the woman as she ran her hands through Katalya's hair.

"What?"

"In your hair ... it's greasy."

A tear ran down her cheek. "It's oil." The vision of Mori popped into her consciousness and she began to weep.

"Stop that!" demanded the woman as she began to scrub Katalya's hair.

Katalya's body began to convulse with sobs.

"No decent merchant will buy a crier," warned the woman, grabbing Katalya's arm. "Do you want to work in a shop or the mines?"

Katalya looked vacantly into the woman's eyes.

"Well if you don't stop that bawling, you're gonna end up a kilometer underground in the dark. Is that what you want?"

Sucking in deep breaths of air as she tried to calm herself, Katalya nodded in acknowledgement.

"Good," said the woman.

A splash of cold water shot straight through her bones as the woman emptied a bucket over Katalya's head.

"Move on," ordered the woman.

Katalya stepped in front of the next woman.

"Arms up."

She complied and raised her arms so the woman could slide a plain tan dress over her body. The coarse material rubbed against her as the bottom fell to mid-thigh.

"Now for the pants," said the woman. "The dress is so they can see you are a girl and the pants are so they see you as a worker."

Katalya stepped into a pair of black, thin-fiber pants and pulled them to her waist.

"Shoes."

She slid her feet into a pair of leather sandals.

"Good. Next!" shouted the woman as she motioned for the next girl.

Katalya walked toward the last woman who was standing at a door opposite the one from which she had entered.

"What can you do?" asked the woman.

"What?"

"Are you fast, strong ... do you sing? How many languages do you speak? What makes you special?"

Katalya stood silent, confused by the questioning.

The woman frowned. "Or do you want to go to the mines?"

"I can dance," blurted Katalya. "And I speak Akota, Standard Terillian, and the trade language."

"I know you can speak the trade language, girl ... since you're talking to me."

"And I —"

"That's enough," interrupted the woman as a yellow light illuminated above the door. "When you go into the next room just do as you are told."

The light turned green and the woman opened the door.

Katalya stepped through the open door and onto a bright stage. Below the stage were dozens of people holding electronic ledgers.

"Step onto the block," came a voice from her left.

Katalya turned to see a middle-aged woman in a long, tight red dress.

"Here," continued the woman, directing her hand toward a platform in the center of the stage.

Katalya, squinting as her eyes adjusted to the light, stepped onto the block.

"Ladies and gentlemen," said the woman, "our next item is a young Terillian girl in excellent health. She speaks Terillian, Akota, and the trade language so she would be useful in many shop applications.

Katalya watched as people began to punch keys on their ledgers.

"Stepdown and come over here," said the woman.

She stepped down from the block and walked over to a stack of metal weights.

"Pick up as many as you can," ordered the woman.

Katalya looked down toward the pile of metal.

"Go ahead, girl."

Katalya began to pick up the metal bars and stack them in her arms until they began to block her view.

"That's enough, girl," said the woman, "put them down."

Katalya knelt and placed the metal bars back onto the floor.

"Not only is she strong," said the woman in the dress, "but she is also a trained dancer ... a welcome bonus to anyone who entertains."

The woman pointed toward a door at the left of the stage. "Okay. Over there."

A guard opened the door when Katalya reached it.

"Come on," directed the guard as she stepped inside, grabbing her arm and pulling her through a tight passageway.

Katalya struggled to keep pace with the guard as he hurried her toward an elevator at the far end of the hallway.

The door opened.

"Get in," ordered the guard.

Katalya stepped into the elevator and the door closed behind her.

Her strength left her and she crumpled to the floor in the corner of the elevator as it began to descend. Curled into a tight ball, she began to shake.

She was completely alone.

The elevator door opened.

"Out you go," came a man's voice.

Katalya glanced up from the floor to see a small, round man dressed similarly to the one Tamar had given her to at the entrance.

"Hurry now."

Katalya pulled herself to her feet and stepped out of the elevator into what seemed to be a series of holding cells.

The man grabbed her arm and ran a scanner over the tracker that had been implanted in her arm.

"Already sold," he said. "No holding bin for you," he continued, glancing toward a nearby guard. "Take this one to loading dock 10-A for transfer."

And just like that, she had gone from daughter and sister to someone's property.

Chapter 5

"Katalya!" shouted Virginia Dak-ori. "Get another case of wine from the back."

"Yes, V," replied Katalya, shouting over the rumble of conversations and the blaring music in the bar.

In the four years since she'd been sold into slavery, she had done what her mother had told her and not caused trouble. And she had been lucky; Virginia Dak-ori had bought Katalya to work at her bar, Dak's Dive, one of the countless bars dotting the villages and mining towns on the great plains of Sierra 7.

Virginia was nothing like family but had rarely beaten Katalya. "No need to break your own shit," she had always said. Virginia had also provided Katalya a warm place to sleep on a cot in the bar's storage room and made sure she didn't go too hungry.

Over the same time, Katalya had grown steadily. At almost 165 cm and still growing, she had transitioned from a frightened girl into an energetic young woman. But perhaps too much a woman. She had to work hard to hide her body — she kept her hair short and unkempt and for the last year, she had bound her chest every morning in hopes everyone would see her as a laborer and nothing else.

"Scoot," added Virginia.

Katalya hustled to the back and made her way to the shelf of wine next to her cot. Running her hands over the labels on the shelf, she stopped on the first one labeled 'Already Watered.' Pulling the label off the box, she picked it up and headed toward the bar.

"Here, V," huffed Katalya, setting the case on the bar. "Want me to stock them?"

"No. Go over there and take those guys' orders."

"But V, you know I —"

"That's enough backtalk, girl. You do as I say and get over there.

"Yes, V," replied Katalya, grabbing an electronic tablet from the bar.

Katalya hated working the floor; she was always more comfortable moving stock or doing the cleaning. The floor was a frightening place for her. It was full of drunk miners, merchants out with their mistresses, and men like the ones that had destroyed her world four years ago.

Three men sat at the table. The man facing the bar was older with gray hair but well dressed. The second man was in his mid-thirties with dark hair and a thick beard. He had a strong build and she caught a glimpse of a pistol on the man's vest. The third was facing away from her but she could see he wore an expensive gray suit and that his hair was well-groomed.

Katalya's heart pounded as she walked to the table. '*At least they're not slavers*,' she thought to herself.

"Can I help you?" asked Katalya.

The men looked up toward her. Their gazes felt like fire on her skin.

"Yes," replied the older man facing her. "A bottle of your best wine," he added.

"I'll have water," said the man in the expensive gray suit.

The man turned slightly to speak to Katalya. He had bright blue eyes and a blocked jaw covered by a thin beard. "I like a clear head when negotiating," he said with a smile. He paused. "How old are you, girl?"

"Almost seventeen," she replied.

"And you work as waitress?"

"I do stock and cleaning mostly," she answered.

"A laborer?" he asked. "Very unusual," posed the man. "And how long have you been here."

"Four years," she answered, growing more uncomfortable. "I should get your order in."

"Of course, girl," said the man.

Katalya scampered to the bar and grabbed a bottle of wine from the case she had brought out from the back. Next, she grabbed four glasses, filling one with water. She closed her eyes and shook her head before picking up the tray. After a deep breath, she headed toward the table.

When she reached the men, Katalya began placing glasses on the table.

"Where are you from?" asked the man in the gray suit.

"I am Akota," she replied.

"And do you like your job?" asked the man in Akota.

Katalya paused. It had been so long she had heard her native tongue. "Yes," replied Katalya in Akota. "Are you?"

"No," said the man with a laugh. "I am from the Bravo system … but it never hurts to be able to talk to people in their native tongue."

"It's nice to hear," replied Katalya, still uncomfortable but forcing a smile.

The man returned her smile.

"I'm sorry," said Katalya, "but I must get back."

"Of course. I was nice to meet you, miss …"

"My name is Katalya."

"Nice to meet you Katalya."

***

The sound of the supply room door opening startled Katalya out of her sleep. She raised up to see Virginia standing over her.

"You need to get dressed," said Virginia firmly. "And no talking back."

Katalya could tell by the scowl on Virginia's face that she meant it. The few times she had seen that look, a beating had followed any time she had not done exactly as she was told.

"Okay, V," replied Katalya, standing and reaching for her pants.

"Not that," said Virginia, extending a red dress toward Katalya. "And don't put that damn binding on either."

"I don't —" She stopped. "Yes, V," she said, taking the dress in her hands.

"Well, put it on."

Katalya's heart raced as she slid the dress over her head.

"Pull," said Virginia.

Katalya let out a slight grunt as she pulled the tight, elastic dress down her body. Once it was on, she continued to tug at the hem of the short, tight dress.

"That's as far as it goes," said Virginia, stepping back and looking at Katalya. "You really are a pretty one."

Katalya had grown to both hate and fear the word pretty. Nothing good came of being pretty if you were a slave. The tight dress, hugging her body like a second skin, felt like a noose.

"Please, V," pleaded Katalya. "Tell me what this is about."

"It's about you making some real money for me, girl."

"I can work harder. I promise," begged Katalya.

"Not enough," said Virginia.

"But —"

"Look, kid. You're a hard worker and haven't given me too much trouble, but frankly I should have done this two years ago."

"Please," sobbed Katalya. Her breathing grew heavy. "What did I do?"

"You grew up, girl … and I need the money. But don't worry, I set you up with a real nice guy … they'll be no recreation house for you."

"What … where …"

"Bravo-3 will be your new home. You just need to be nice to the man outside."

"No," replied Katalya, "I just —"

"Maybe I didn't make myself clear, Katalya," interrupted Virginia. "I need the money ... so if you ruin it for me with this guy ..." She paused, grabbing Katalya's arms. "... then you will go to a recreation house."

"Please." Her body trembled as she shook her head. "I'll do anything —"

"You will do whatever Mr. Xiang tells you. You are his now."

Katalya couldn't speak. She let out little gasps as she struggled to breathe. "I —"

"He's waiting," interrupted Virginia, wiping Katalya's tears with a rag.

Katalya's thoughts flashed back to the last moments with her mother and the advice she had given her.

"Okay," huffed Katalya, catching her breath.

"Good," said Virginia as she turned and walked to the door.

Virginia opened the door and Katalya stepped through, her head fixed on the floor. She took a few feet and stopped.

"Come now, Katalya," said Virginia, "Introduce yourself to Mr. Xiang."

Katalya slowly raised her head. In front of her stood the same well-dressed man that had spoken to her earlier that night. Next to him was the large man in dark heavy cloak.

"Good evening, Katalya," said the man with a smile.

Katalya subconsciously took a step backwards only to feel the pressure of Virginia's hand on her back.

"Say hello, girl," said Virginia through her teeth, shoving Katalya forward.

"Hello, Mr. Xiang," she said, almost at a whisper.

"She's shy," offered Virginia, her face tight with anxiousness. "But I'm sure once —

Mr. Xiang silenced Virginia with a raised hand.

"It's okay," he said, slowly walking to Katalya. "You have nothing to fear from me, Katalya," he said with a smile as he gently placed her right hand between his. "I am confident you will find your new life very satisfying."

Katalya stared at her feet, afraid if she looked up that it would be real.

Mr. Xiang's hand cupped her lower jaw, gently raising her head until their eyes met. Even though his eyes looked calm, almost soothing, her body still shook with distress.

"Is everything okay, Mr. Xiang?" asked Virginia.

"Oh, yes," replied Xiang. "Everything is fine."

"Then if we can?" asked Virginia, holding out a ledger pad.

Mr. Xiang took the ledger from Virginia and pressed the keypad. "Transaction complete."

"Thank you, Mr. Xiang," said Virginia. "I'm sure you'll be happy with the deal."

"I already am," replied Xiang with a glance and a smile towards Katalya. "Very much so."

Katalya turned toward Virginia, tears welling in her eyes.

"It'll be okay, kid," said Virginia. "You'll probably be better off."

"Come, Katalya," said Xiang, extending a hand. "I can promise you that you will be better off."

Katalya slowly raised her hand and Xiang took her hand in a calm, but firm grasp.

***

Katalya stared at the wall as she sat in the plush cabin of a transport ship. She had done little but exist over the last four years and now she wished for nothing but to be on that cot in the stock room.

"We'll be taking off soon," said Xiang, kneeling in front of her.

Katalya nodded her head but didn't speak.

"I know this is a lot of change for you, sweet Katalya, but before you know it things will be better."

Xiang placed two pills in Katalya's hand.

"Take them."

She sensed his hand on her knee and jerked away from him.

"Don't be startled, Katalya," he said, moving his hand away. "I want to make sure you're comfortable … these will help you sleep during the trip."

She looked at the pills and then glanced up toward Xiang.

"Take them," he said, "I promise they will not harm you."

"And if I don't want to?"

He smiled and placed his hand to her cheek. "You will take them, Katalya."

She slowly raised her hand to take the pills from Xiang's hand. She had no choice and knew it.

"There you go," said Xiang, watching Katalya take the pills and place them in her mouth.

Katalya swallowed hard to force the pills down her throat.

"See," said Xiang. "Now you will rest," he said as he stood. "By the time we arrive at my estate, you will see that being my concubine will be a good thing."

Chapter 6

Katalya slowly opened her eyes.

She looked up toward the overhead and took a deep breath. Still groggy from the pills Xiang had given her, she slowly pushed herself into a sitting position. After another breath, she ran her hands over her head. Her eyes opened wide when she felt long, smooth hair where a short, choppy mess had been before.

"I hope you slept well."

Katalya looked to her right to see Xiang standing above her.

"My hair?"

"Oh yes. That was the second pill … we can't have a beautiful girl like you with the hair of a little boy, can we?"

Katalya said nothing.

"And there's no reason to wait for it grow when we can help it along," continued Xiang.

She pulled her hair in front of her face and let it fall. It was now longer than it had been before she was captured.

"Do you like it?"

She looked up toward Xiang.

"Do you like it?" he repeated, sitting next to her and running his hand through her hair to the small of her back.

She closed her eyes and took a deep breath, fighting her churning stomach. Not knowing what else to do, she nodded.

"Very good," said Xiang, standing. "I am sure you must be hungry."

"I am," she replied.

"Well then, Katalya, you may clean yourself in my chambers ... in the next room aft. You will also find more clothing for you there as well. Once you are ready, please join me in the forward compartment for dinner."

Again she nodded.

She pushed herself to her feet and walked a few meters to Xiang's chambers. She stopped in front of the scanner. There was a chirp and the word 'Authorized' flashed on the screen.

The door slid open and she stepped inside. Inside the bedchamber was a large bed with multiple pillows and blankets ... more than she had seen on any bed in her life, especially compared to the cot where she had slept for the last four years. To the right was a dark wooden desk with black accents in the wood.

She walked to the bed and ran her hand over the blankets. They were softer than anything she had felt before. At the foot of the bed lay a black cheongsam dress with golden flower accents. She ran her fingers over the dress, finding that it was softer than the blanket. Looking up from the dress, she saw a small but ornate shower and a deep ceramic tub in a small room with glass doors.

After a quick glance toward the entrance to make sure the door had closed, she slid her tight red dress over her shoulders and rolled it over her hips. Pushing it down to her feet, she stepped out of the dress and opened the door to the shower. The water was cold but after the shock, she welcomed how it made her feel … numb.

As the water slowly warmed, she began to cry.

***

"Come, Katalya," said Xiang, "join me for dinner."

A shiver ran down her spine as Xiang's hand touched the small of her back.

"It's just dinner," said Xiang, sensing her nervousness.

She nodded, forcing a smile.

"You should smile more. It suits you."

Not knowing how to respond, Katalya began to walk toward the dining compartment. As she did, she sensed the constant pressure of Xiang's hand on her back.

The door to the dining chamber opened. At the door stood a thin, pale man in formal black pants and a button-up white shirt underneath a black vest.

"Good evening, Sir," said the man as he turned toward Katalya. "And good evening, Miss Katalya. I am Annon, Mr. Xiang's shuttle servant."

"Good evening, Annon," replied Katalya.

Annon bowed slightly and stepped to his right. As Annon stepped aside, Katalya took in the feast set out before her. Fruits and vegetables, some of which she had never seen before, were neatly organized on the side table to her left. To the right were several cooked meats, enough to feed a dozen men. The smell of the food flooded her senses, causing her stomach to tighten in a confusing combination of anticipation and anxiety.

"There's so much food," she said aloud.

"Every day will be like this," replied Xiang.

She felt Xiang's hand on the small of her back again as he directed her toward the main.

"Miss Katalya," said Annon with a smile as he pulled out her chair.

She slowly lowered herself on the chair and allowed Annon to gently slide the chair toward the table. Katalya glanced up toward Xiang. No one had ever pulled out a chair for her … or called her 'Miss.'

"You may be my servant, Katalya, but most of my servants will treat you as their superior due to your position in the household." He paused, placing his hand on her shoulder. "But we will have plenty of time to discuss house rules later."

"Thank you," said Katalya.

"That won't be necessary, Katalya," said Xiang. "He is expected to serve you … as you serve me."

Katalya's gaze shifted downward toward the table.

"Do you understand?" he asked, sitting across from her.

She looked up toward Xiang. He had a pleasant, relaxed look about him, but Katalya knew he was asking if she knew her place.

"Yes, Mr. Xiang."

"Splendid. Now we shall eat," he replied, waving for Annon to begin the meal service.

"Very well, Sir," replied Annon. "What shall you have, Sir?"

"The lady will go first, Annon."

"Of course, Sir," replied Annon, turning toward Katalya. "Miss?"

"Uh …" She could not remember the last time she had a choice of food. "I just … can you pick for me?"

"Do not ask, Katalya," interrupted Xiang. "Tell him."

"Yes, Mr. Xiang," she replied quietly, "you choose for me."

"Very good," replied Xiang, taking her plate and handing it to Annon.

She watched as Annon placed two different meats, a variety of greens, and an assortment of fruits on her plate.

"And your drink, Miss Katalya?"

"Water, pleas — water," she replied.

"She will also have some wine," added Xiang

Katalya watched Xiang as Annon poured her wine. He looked so pleased, like a child teaching a new pet tricks.

"And you, Sir?" asked Annon after filling Katalya's glass.

"I will have my usual, Annon," replied Xiang, his gaze locked on Katalya. "So Katalya, shall we discuss what you can expect when we arrive at my estate?"

"If you wish, Mr. Xiang."

"Excellent." Xiang paused to take a drink of wine, motioning for Katalya to do the same. "We will arrive at my estate on Bravo-3 in two standard weeks. Once there, you will first be introduced to Charles, my head administrator. He will go over all of the rules in detail. After that, you will be introduced to Mrs. Xiang."

"You have a wife?"

Xiang took in a quick breath and exhaled slowly, showing just the slightest bit of annoyance. "Yes, Katalya. Our customs are different than what you may be used to … but you will learn. Mrs. Xiang must always be treated with respect; never start or seek conversation with her. Any concerns or problems will be relayed through Charles. Is that clear?"

"Yes, Mr. Xiang."

"Good. So, once you are introduced to Mrs. Xiang, Charles will then show you to your house."

"House?"

"Yes. You will have a house on the estate separate from the main structure. You will also have a servant to help you and Charles will check in with you daily. Other than that, or times when you are with me, you should not interact with others on the estate, nor should they with you."

"I cannot leave the estate?"

"Of course you can," replied Xiang with a smile. "I will escort you off the estate several times a year." He took another drink. "I will also make every effort to maintain a schedule, of which Charles will keep you informed, so that you can adequately prepare."

"Prepare?" she asked. But she knew what he meant.

"Yes. For the nights I will stay with you."

Katalya looked down toward the table again.

"Do not worry, you are young and nervous about such things but that will not last long."

She felt his hand grip hers.

"Do you not think so?" he continued.

"Yes, Mr. Xiang," she replied, unable to look up from the table.

"Excellent," said Xiang, his lips curled in a half-smile. "I think that is enough about that. Let's enjoy this meal."

Katalya stared at her plate. Her stomach churned from a combination of hunger and anxiety over what she had become. She would apparently be offered comforts the likes of which she had never seen, but the price would be her body.

***

Katalya stared at her empty plate.

"Was the meal pleasing?" asked Xiang.

"Yes, Mr. Xiang. Thank you."

"I'm glad you enjoyed it," replied Xiang. "I'm sure you would like to relax now.

"If you wish," she said, almost at a whisper.

"Annon, please show Miss Katalya back to my chambers and ensure that she is comfortable. I will be making several communications and will need to be undisturbed."

"Yes, Sir," replied Annon, turning toward Katalya. "Please follow me."

Katalya slowly rose and followed Annon back to Xiang's chambers. As they entered, Annon walked to a bureau and pulled out a long silk gown.

"Here, Miss Katalya. You should change into this after I leave. Is there anything else I may do for you?"

She felt her meal begin to churn inside her stomach. Annon could probably get her anything she asked for, except for the one thing she wanted — her freedom.

"No."

"Very well, Miss Katalya," replied Annon, turning to leave.

"Wait. Annon…"

"Yes, Ma'am?"

"What am I supposed to do?" she asked, almost begging.

Annon placed his hand on her shoulder. "Mr. Xiang is generally a kind man," he said with a smile that quickly faded. "You are supposed to do what we are all supposed to do … what you are told."

With that, Annon left the room.

Katalya looked down at the silk robe lying on the bed. Her mind flashed back to her mother before she was ripped from her hands. 'Survive,' echoed through her mind as she picked up the robe.

***

Katalya sat on the edge of the bed, the thin silk robe sending tickling sensations all over her skin. The soft caress of the silk was contrasted by the pounding of her heart.

The door opened. Startling her.

"Sorry for taking so long," said Xiang. "But business must come before pleasure."

Every rapid beat of her heart felt like an explosion in her chest. Her stomach tightened.

"I see you have put the robe on. Do you like it?"

"Yes, Mr. Xiang." Her hands gripped the bed sheet tightly as she stared at the floor.

She winced slightly when his hand touched her hair and slowly moved down to her cheek. She tried to calm herself, but her body trembled.

"Now, now," said Xiang in a reassuring tone as she raised her head toward him. "There is nothing to fear."

"Yes, Mr. Xiang," she replied, her voice cracking.

"Come. Stand and let me see you," said Xiang, gently pulling on her arm.

Although she thought her legs would buckle, she slowly stood. As she did, Xiang placed his hands under her chin, cupping her jaw gently. "Beautiful," he said, sliding his hands down her shoulders.

She felt him brush the robe off her shoulders.

It fell to the floor.

The air on her naked body sent a chill down her spine. Her body exposed, she again looked toward the floor.

"It's okay, Katalya," he said, again directing her to look into his eyes. "This does not have to be a bad experience. You were chosen because you are beautiful. It is that beauty that will provide you with safety and comfort for years to come."

His hand slowly ran over her shoulder and down her arm as he leaned in to kiss her neck gently.

The soft touch of his lips against her skin sent a sensation shooting through her body. Her stomach still churned but a new sensation — a tingling — began to grow in another part of her body. She did not want him to touch her. That is what her head and heart told her, but her body was alert and tense in a way she had never felt before.

"Are you not happy with what I have provided for you?"

"Yes, Mr. Xiang," she replied with a heavy breath as his hand moved back up her side, pulling her body close to his. Her mind raced as a myriad of emotions and sensations flooded her consciousness.

She closed her eyes.

She sensed her feet leaving the ground as Xiang picked her up and placed her on the bed.

She opened her eyes.

She looked up toward him as he positioned himself on top of her.

She closed her eyes again.

Chapter 7

Katalya stood trembling in the massive parlor of Xiang's main house with Xiang and Annon by her side. The meticulously maintained gardens, dotted with ponds and streams running past them, were nothing compared to the marble floors, vaulted ceilings, and ornate tapestries of the main house.

"Mr. Xiang," said a tall man in black pants and a red tunic who entered the room. "I am glad to see you returned safe from your travels." He took a long look at Katalya. "And that your search was successful."

"Thank you, Charles," replied Xiang.

"Mr. Xiang, I must inform you that Mrs. Xiang is ready for the introductions."

"Before you provide the necessary instructions?"

"Yes, Mr. Xiang."

"Very well, Charles," huffed Xiang. "I am sure Katalya will do well."

Charles pressed a button on a keypad attached to his wrist.

Two young women in long, decorative silk robes walked into the room, stopping in front of Katalya and the others.

"Mrs. Xiang's attendants," whispered Annon. "She's coming."

Katalya tried to slow her breathing to calm herself but it didn't help.

One of the attendants rang a small bell in her hands and Mrs. Corina Xiang stepped into the room from behind a sliding canvas door covered in another ornate tapestry. In her late thirties or early forties, she was still stunning. Her jet-black hair was tied into a single three-weave braid that almost touched the floor. She wore a long emerald green dress with a wide yellow and white sash that fit tightly around her slim waste.

Katalya's eyes stayed locked on her as she slowly walked across the floor and stopped in front of her husband. Her amber eyes flickered like candles against the thin white coating of makeup on her face.

Katalya bowed to Corina as Annon had taught her during their transit. "I am very pleased to meet, Mrs. Xiang, and humbly present myself as a member of your household."

"Rise," said Corina dryly, her gaze still locked on her husband. "So this is her?"

"Yes, Corina," replied Xiang.

"She will make you look good with the other landed nobles," continued Corina, turning toward Katalya. "Very pretty indeed."

"And her presence will increase the prestige of the house you oversee, dear."

"Yes. That is why I agreed to this," said Corina, turning back to Xiang. "She may go now," she added without looking at Katalya. You may have your man show the concubine to her quarters."

"Yes, Ma'am," replied Charles, turning toward Katalya. "This way, girl."

"And Charles," added Corina, causing Katalya to stop and look back toward her. When their eyes met, Katalya could feel the hatred radiate from Corina. Her gaze felt like a cloak wrapping around Katalya's body. "Make sure she understands her place," she added before turning and walking out of the room.

"Of course, Ma'am," replied Charles as Corina left the room. "Now, Miss Katalya," he spoke, "follow me."

***

With Charles at her side, Katalya walked down a small stone pathway through a lavish garden. After a few meters, she spoke.

"She hates me."

"Of course she does, girl," replied Charles. "You are her husband's new plaything, and all wives hate the new ones until they are sure they will not be replaced. Then she will ignore you, if you are lucky. In a few months she will most likely look at you no differently than one of the master's hogs or cattle," he said matter-of-factly. "If you're lucky."

Katalya stopped. "And if I'm unlucky?"

"Then you will wish you were one of the master's hogs or cattle," he replied with a slight tug on her arm. "Now come."

They continued down the pathway.

"I assume Annon discussed the basics of behavior with you?"

"Yes. Except for you, Mr. Xiang, and his family, I am to expect to be served by the others and —"

"Yes," interrupted Charles, "but even if you grow to enjoy it, act like you do not when the Xiang's are not around. The other servants will be jealous and undoubtedly dislike you."

"Then —"

"But do not allow them to disrespect you. If you do, you will lose any leverage with them and anger the master."

"I understand," she replied although she didn't understand anything about her new world.

"Good … now for Mrs. Xiang. You will never enter the main household unless summoned by myself or are in the company of Mr. Xiang. The household belongs to Mrs. Xiang and for you to be there uninvited would be an act of disrespect to her."

"I understand."

"Also, when you are in the main household, address her as Mrs. Xiang or Madame Xiang. Do not say anything to her unless spoken to and then give her only direct answers."

"Yes."

"And do not touch Mr. Xiang in the household. He may touch you and you may reciprocate but do not initiate contact with him in the main house. That is what your private chamber is for … do you understand?"

"I do." She wished she didn't.

"Excellent," replied Charles, stopping at a small wooden fence. "And we are here."

Charles opened the gate to a small one-story cottage. Despite its size, it was well made with dark spruce siding and a roof angled slightly downward from the center.

"This is mine?" she asked. She couldn't remember a time when she had more room than a cot and a small locker for her belongings.

"It is Mr. Xiang's, as are you, girl," replied Charles. "But you will reside here," he added, opening the door.

Inside stood a young girl who was not much older than Katalya had been when she was taken from her mother. The girl wore plain, but well-kept gray trousers and a matching button-up collarless shirt. Her long blonde hair was tied in a braid that ran over her shoulder and almost to her waist.

She bowed.

"Good evening, Miss Katalya," she squeaked. "I am Dari and I will be your attendant."

As the girl spoke, Katalya noticed a large scar running down the side of her face.

"Dari's family escaped the Civil Wars on the Southern Hemisphere, but her family needed money for transport off-planet so they made a trade with Mr. Xiang," said Charles.

Katalya's heart sank. She remembered how much her family had fought for her — and Dari's had traded her for a transport ticket.

"Her scar made her unusable in most of the rec houses, so Mr. Xiang was kind enough to keep her on as a servant," added Charles.

"Shall I show you the house, Miss Katalya?" asked Dari.

Katalya stood silent, still trying to understand how parents could give away one of their children.

"Don't worry about me," said Dari. "It's not too bad here. Much better than being stuck in the fighting in the South."

"Dari," said Charles. "Show Katalya to her bed chamber and then prepare her some dinner."

"Yes, Mr. Charles," replied Dari.

Charles turned toward Katalya. "The master will not see you tonight. He will spend the next three days with his wife."

"Yes," said Katalya, a wave of relief passing over her.

"But on the fourth night you will be prepared to receive him for dinner ... and for the night."

"Yes," she replied.

"Very well then." Charles turned toward Dari. "Dari, do as you are told and help Miss Katalya with the rules."

"Yes, Mr. Charles."

"What do you want to see next?" asked Dari after Charles closed the door behind him.

"I don't know."

"Then I will show you everything."

Katalya nodded and Dari took her arm to lead her through the cottage.

"Here's the main dining area," said Dari, pointing to a small round table with two chairs. "This is where you and the master will have meals."

"Where do you eat?" asked Katalya.

"Oh, I don't eat at the table, Miss Katalya. There is a small counter in the kitchen over here where I eat."

Katalya followed Dari past the small round table and through a curtain of colorful beads which were arranged to make the shape of a mountain with green fields below. On the other side was a cramped kitchen with just enough room for some storage and cooking.

"When Mr. Xiang is here, he will pick the meals, but you can decide the rest of the time."

Katalya glanced over to a small counter with a half-eaten bowl of rice on it.

"You can sit at the table with me when he isn't here," said Katalya.

Dari spun around. "Oh no, Miss Katalya. I can't. You are the master's mistress. You must eat alone or with him."

Katalya could tell by Dari's reaction there was no use talking to her about it.

"Outside," continued Dari, "is a small garden for you to relax. If you like, I can get some books for you or have one of the musicians come and play for you if they aren't busy in the main house."

Katalya looked through the small window in the kitchen to see a small, well-kept garden full of colorful flowers and meticulously trimmed trees. At the center were two wooden benches surrounding a pond fed by a small stream. It was so beautiful she almost forgot she was a slave.

"Now I will show you the bedroom where you and Mr. Xiang will …" She paused, snickering. "… do stuff."

The small bit of solace created by the garden evaporated.

"Come on," said Dari, waving.

Katalya followed Dari back past the dining table and through the foyer to another beaded curtain. Dari stopped at the curtain and parted it at the center. The bedroom was the largest room in the house. Inside was a large pedestal bed with two reading chairs and a series of ornate wooden doors on the wall to her right.

"This is where your clothes are," said Dari, opening the doors to show several drawers and two long rows of dresses. "And here is your shower."

Katalya looked to her left to a large stone shower leading to a deep tub.

"Plenty of room for you and the master," said Dari with a smile.

"Where do you sleep?" asked Katalya wanting to change the subject.

Dari pointed to a door in the far corner of the room. "I have a small shack just outside. All you need to do is push any of the silver buttons on the intercoms and it rings in my room. Push the red one and I will stay out until you push it again. You can use it whenever you want to be alone ... or when the master is visiting and you don't want me —"

"I understand," interrupted Katalya.

She took a deep breath. Was this to be her life? Despite the comforts, she had become the sex slave of a Dark Zone lord. She felt her heart sink as her thoughts drifted to her family. She thought about Mori — she was still out there somewhere, or at least Katalya liked to think she was.

"Are you okay, Miss Katalya?" asked Dari.

Katalya looked down toward Dari, her eyes moving to the scar on the girl's face.

"You sure are lucky, Miss Katalya," said Dari with a smile.

Katalya wondered which fate, hers or Dari's, she would rather have.

"I'm okay," she said, forcing a smile to her face. "I just need some rest.

Chapter 8

Katalya stared at the ceiling. She had been at Xiang's estate for several months, but on some nights, mostly those when Xiang would visit, sleep escaped her.

Xiang's body shifted next to hers and she felt the pressure of his hand on her stomach.

"That was pleasant," he said with a smile, his hand sliding over her hip.

"I'm glad you are pleased," she replied, still staring at the ceiling.

"I have a new dress for you," he added, placing his hand on her cheek and turning her head toward him. "We will be traveling tomorrow and I want you to wear it."

"Of course, Mr. Xiang."

"And I want you to be on your best behavior. This is an important meeting of nobles and I want everyone to be jealous."

"Have I not behaved well on other trips?" she asked. "If I have in some way —"

"No, Katalya," laughed Xiang. "You have always been a joy." He leaned forward and kissed her gently. "I am just nervous. This is a very important meeting."

"I will act only to bring you honor, Mr. Xiang."

"And watch out for the other nobles' mistresses," said Xiang, a stern look coming over his face. "They are gossipy, manipulative things."

She placed her hand on his check. By now she had learned how to calm him — most of the time. "I know my place," she said with a reassuring smile.

"You are the best business decision I have ever made," he replied, kissing her again.

He had no idea how his compliments only made her feel even more a piece of property.

"Thank you," she said, forcing a smile. "And I will show the others how a nobleman's woman should behave."

She kissed him softly on his lips.

A smile came to his face before he rolled onto his side, his back to her.

She rolled onto her back, taking a deep breath and staring at the ceiling again.

***

Katalya smiled at Xiang, his hand slowly moving up and down her thigh as the two sat at a large table full of nobles and their mistresses.

"Your concubine is exquisite," said Dzu Yang, Xiang's political rival for control of the Northeastern Provinces. "So refined."

"She was quite a find," replied Xiang, giving Katalya's thigh a squeeze.

Katalya bowed her head in acknowledgment of the compliment but as she raised her head, she saw Yang's mistress glaring at her. The woman, in her early thirties, was beautiful despite the slightest hint of age showing in the corner of her eyes. Her scarlet hair was tied in a tight bun with two thin tufts running down her cheeks. Her gaze still looked on Katalya, she took a drink and spoke.

"A girl as pretty as her must have been in high demand at the recreation house," said Yang's mistress. "She must have cost you dearly."

"Regina!" growled Yang. "It is not appropriate to say such things."

Katalya glanced at Xiang. He was eating up the social misstep of Yang's concubine.

"She is not from a recreation house," replied Xiang. "She was pure when I acquired her."

She saw the head of every man at the table snap toward her. She could almost feel their thoughts crawling on her skin.

"Pure, you say?" asked Fan Yi, the regional magistrate. "How fortunate."

"It is I who was fortunate," said Katalya. She may have felt like a piece of meat, but she knew the better she made Xiang look, the better off she would be in the long run.

"Well said, Miss Katalya," said Yang, casting a disapproving glance at Regina. "You honor your master."

Again she nodded in acknowledgment.

This time when she raised her head, all of the mistresses were shooting daggers at her with their eyes. But her life wasn't determined by them; Xiang was the only one that mattered.

"Perhaps you should get me another drink," said Yang to Regina, tapping on his almost-empty glass.

"I could use one as well," added Yi to his mistress.

Katalya rose and took Xiang's glass in her hand. "I will get you a drink as well, Mr. Xiang."

After giving Xiang a smile, she turned and walked across the room to a small bar. On the way to the bar, neither girl spoke to her — or looked at her. Reaching the bar, she gave Xiang's glass to the bartender and kept her gaze locked straight ahead.

"Make it a double," said Regina to the bartender before turning to Yi's mistress. "He's pissed so I need to make sure he passes out as soon as we get back to the room … I don't want to deal with that tonight."

"Well at least he's not sixty years old," replied Yi's mistress with a glance toward her aged master. He saw her and smiled. As she turned back, her smile transitioned to a scowl. "Image that crawling on top of you."

"Better one old man a few times a week than twenty smelly miners and soldiers every day," retorted Regina.

"True," replied Yi's mistress. "We can't all get a young, fit one like Mr. Xiang," she added, turning toward Katalya.

"That must be a fun ride," said Yi's woman.

Katalya must have shown the slightest hint of embarrassment, causing Regina to tilt her head.

"You really were pure," she said.

"I was," replied Katalya, looking toward the floor.

"No shit," laughed Yi's woman. "Aren't you just the luckiest little bitch," she snarled. "No time in the rec house … and you get a nice young master."

Katalya couldn't comprehend how someone could be so jealous of her situation,

72

but both women glared at her as if she had stolen something from them.

"Oh, well," said Regina. "I bet the wife hates you."

"I stay away from Mrs. Xiang unless Mr. Xiang requests me in the main house."

"Aren't you just the perfect little robot fuck doll," said Regina with a dry smile.

"Xiang must just lap you up," added Yi's mistress.

"Just watch," added Regina to Yi's mistress. "So young and pretty … she'll wrap Xiang around her little finger and he'll try to replace his wife with her." Regina turned toward Katalya. "If his wife even thinks for a second that will happen, she'll have you snatched up when he is off on business."

"If that happens," added Yi's mistress, "you'll be lucky to end up in a third-rate rec house servicing miners on paydays."

"Lucky?" Katalya didn't even realize she had asked.

"Yes," replied Regina. "You're more likely to end up all carved up and dumped in some ravine in the wastelands."

"Mr. Xiang would not allow that," she replied, defending Xiang out of fear they might be right. "And Mrs. Xiang is too traditional to do that."

"Oh, honey," laughed Regina. "That is tradition. Nobles' wives have been making little bitches like you disappear for generations."

"Watch this one end up the queen of Xiang's household though," replied Yi's mistress with a smirk. "All fancy and proper."

"Well I ain't calling you Lady Katalya. That's for damn sure," said Regina.

"We should get back," said Katalya, wanting to get away from the toxic duo. "Mr. Xiang is waiting … as are your masters."

"Hmmm," mouthed Yi's mistress.

Katalya quickly grabbed Xiang's drink and made her way back to the table.

"Mr. Xiang," she said as she placed the drink in front of him.

"Thank you, Katalya," he replied.

As she sat, Xiang's hand went back to her thigh, squeezing it lightly.

She gave him a quick smile and looked toward the other mistresses returning to the table.

"Where were we?" asked Yi, taking a sip from his new drink.

"The civil war in the South," said Li Fau, another noble at the table. "I think we should support the Red Cloth faction."

"But they are so radicalized," replied Yang. "Unpredictable."

"Their troops and mid-level leaders might be," said Xiang. "But I think this is more evidence of their dedication to their cause. Either way, their upper level leaders are realists. Especially Lord Minister Vlock."

"And they repay their debts," added Fau.

"I had heard the Humani are secretly providing intel and material to the Demos faction," said Yang. "That would mean that supporting the Red Cloth may put us in opposition to Humani interests."

"The Humani are just trying to capitalize on the chaos," replied Xiang. "They couldn't give two shits about what really happens on this planet."

"You might not sound so bold when an Elite Guard team knocks on your door," said Yang.

Katalya had heard her father tell stories of Alpha Humana's most fearless and deadly unit when she was young. They were savages — no better than a pack of wolves.

"Don't let your fear ruin your chance for profit, Yang," said Xiang. "If we support the Red Cloths and they gain the upper hand, then the Humani will support them too. We might even be able to trade with them directly."

"It's risky," replied Yang. "If we —"

"What will it be, Yang," interrupted Xiang, "fear or profit?"

Katalya saw Yang look around the table. Yang couldn't come across as weak, especially in comparison to Xiang.

"Profit," said Yang, lifting his drink above his head.

"To profit," added Xiang, rising his drink as well.

"To profit," echoed the group.

After drinking, Xiang leaned in toward Katalya.

"Thank you," he whispered in her ear. "You really are very special."

***

Katalya felt Xiang's hand squeeze hers as they walked back to her cottage.

He had been unusually affectionate, and not just sexually, toward her the entire two days of their trip as well as their short return home. He had actually begun to ask her about her childhood.

Although the non-sexual attention was a pleasant change, the words of the other mistresses began to echo in her head. Was he beginning to fall for her?

"I want to say again how pleased I am with how you supported me during the trip," he said when they reached the door to her small house. "The way you worked Yang's mistress … it was very useful."

"I'm glad I could help," she replied with a smile.

He leaned in, kissing her. She responded.

"I look forward to your next visit," she said they broke their embrace.

She felt him take her hands into his.

"I will be staying with you tonight."

A bolt of anxiety shot through her body. "But Mrs. Xiang? Isn't it —"

"Charles has been instructed to tell her we have been delayed one more day," he replied, pulling her close and sliding his hands around her waist. "I need to be with my most-prized possession tonight."

Once again, he destroyed any spark of feelings she may have had by referring to her as property.

"As you wish, Mr. Xiang," she replied with a smile although the thought of what Mrs. Xiang might do to her if she found out raced through her mind.

"I like the way that sounds," he replied. "Say it again," he added, sliding his hands over her bottom.

"As you wish, Mr. Xiang."

***

The next morning Katalya sat outside in her garden, watching the ripples in the small pond while Xiang continued to sleep in her bed. She tried not to let herself think about her family, but sometimes she couldn't block out the memories. At least this time they were pleasant ones — memories of times when they were together and happy.

"No," she said aloud, shaking her head. That was a dream, not reality. She had to live in the real world — a world where she was property. She exhaled heavily.

Her head shot upward.

Did she have to be property? Maybe the jaded, jealous mistresses were right about something; Xiang was clearly growing more interested in her every day. If she could make him fall for her, if he wanted her to become his wife, she could regain some sense of freedom. Not true freedom. Not freedom from Xiang. But maybe, as his wife, she could talk him into helping her find her mother and possibly even Mori.

She took another deep breath. She would have to be smart. If Mrs. Xiang found out, she could end up dead if the other mistresses were right.

"Survive," she said to herself, echoing the last words her mother had said to her.

Chapter 9

Katalya stood at the gate leading to the main estate. She knew Xiang would be in the lower garden; he had told her that he would be busy supervising the transplanting of several large trees. And she could hear him giving orders in the distance. She had gradually shown more affection to Xiang over the last few weeks and he had responded by giving her more attention. Xiang had just returned from another meeting of nobles and would be spending the night with his wife. But she knew he would be thinking about her and she needed to take advantage of that.

She took a deep breath and scanned the area for any sign of Mrs. Xiang or her servants. Her heart pounded as she opened the gate and stepped through. If Mrs. Xiang found her on the main estate not in the company of Mr. Xiang, she would be lucky if all she received was a beating.

Katalya quickly made her way through the front garden, sticking close to the fence line as she moved toward the lower garden. In a few moments she was at the edge of the clearing across from where Xiang was working. Peering through the bushes, she could see him pointing toward a large tree being lowered into a hole by a crane as several servants held the tree steady with ropes.

Letting out a puff of air, she stepped into the clearing and walked confidently toward Xiang.

"Slowly," ordered Xiang to the man operating the crane. "You must be gentle. This tree is very del —"

Xiang stopped as he noticed Katalya walking toward him.

A smile came to his face.

She had him.

"Mr. Xiang," she called out as she neared him.

Xiang quickly walked over to her.

"Katalya, why are you here?" he asked. "It isn't appropriate for you to just ..." As he spoke, a smile was still painted on his face.

"I'm sorry, Mr. Xiang," interrupted Katalya. "I just ..." She paused, glancing at the other servants.

They were all watching.

"Get back to work!" ordered Xiang and the servants returned to their tasks.

"I just … I couldn't find Charles and I need to speak with you."

"What is it?"

She looked toward the servants again. "In private … if you would allow it?"

She could see a slight hint of frustration on his face.

"It is very important," she added.

"Very well," replied Xiang, taking her arm. "Let's go over here."

Together they walked to the edge of the heavily wooded portion of garden, just out of sight of the servants.

"What is so —"

Before he could finish, she kissed him forcefully, wrapping her arms around his waist.

"I just needed to be with you," she said, feigning a yearning she would never have for him.

"We shouldn't," he protested although he slid his arms around her. "If Mrs. Xiang were to hear of this …"

She could tell by the pressure of his groin against her hip that although his voice was protesting, his body was not.

"No one will know," she whispered, kissing his neck.

"Katalya!" he growled, taking her cheeks in his hands.

She froze. Had she gone too far in her attempt to seduce him?

She looked into his fierce eyes. "I was —"

This time it was Xiang who silenced her with a kiss. As he kissed her, she felt him lift her into the air. She responded by wrapping her legs around his waist.

She let out a grunt as he pushed her against a tree and slid the robe she was wearing apart.

"Do you want me to take you right here?" he taunted as his hand slid inside her robe.

"You can take me anywhere you like, Master," she huffed, undoing his belt.

She intentionally let out a moan as he entered her.

"Call me Cal," he grunted.

"Cal," she gasped, wrapping her arms around his head as he began to thrust.

Her mind began to drift to another place as she let him have her body; hopefully it would be worth it.

***

"Thank you, Cal," said Katalya, tying her robe tight. "You should get back to the other servants before they wonder where you are," she added.

"You realize you are more than a servant to me, right?" said Xiang, taking her hands into his.

She smiled. "I am here to serve you ... in whatever manner ..." She paused, stepping in close and kissing him gently on the cheek. "... or position you desire."

A content but puzzled expression came over Xiang. "You make me very happy," he said.

"Then I am happy," she replied. "But you must go."

"Of course," said Xiang with a smile.

"Until your next visit," said Katalya, returning Xiang's smile.

"Tonight," he said, almost like a reflex. "After Mrs. Xiang is asleep."

"Tonight," she replied.

Xiang gave her another quick kiss before stepping out of the bushes.

As she watched Xiang walk away Katalya wiped a tear from her cheek. She felt dirty but focused on her family. With a quick breath she started to make her way back to her cottage.

Katalya quickly made her way back to the gate and down the pathway to her cottage. If she played things right —

She stopped in her tracks.

At the gate to her cottage was Mrs. Xiang and two of her male servants.

"Mrs. Xiang," she said, bowing in subservience.

"Where were you, concubine?" asked Mrs. Xiang.

Ice flowed through Katalya's veins as she struggled to take in a breath. "Mrs. Xiang, I ... I —"

Mrs. Xiang slapped Katalya across the face, silencing her. "How dare you?" Mrs. Xiang's face was tight with rage. "I agreed to allow Cal to his little plaything to increase his standing with the other nobles but do not ..." She gripped Katalya's lower jaw with her right hand. "... do not forget your place, trash."

"Mrs. Xiang, I —"

Another open hand landed on Katalya's cheek.

"Silence!" growled Mrs. Xiang. "In case you don't understand your purpose here, it is to be a receptacle for my husband to amuse himself and for him to do things that no lady would allow. You are no better than a piece of meat purchased at the market to be consumed and the leftovers cast out."

Katalya knew better than to speak. She kept her gaze locked on the ground.

"And if you think you can replace me," added Mrs. Xiang, grabbing Katalya's hair and pulling tightly so that she had to look into her eyes. "You will learn two things. First, I am a noblewoman and you are a series of holes for my husband to fill." Katalya felt the two male servants grab her arms, almost lifting her off the ground. Next she felt the cold, hard pressure of a knife against her cheek. "And secondly," continued Mrs. Xiang, "and he won't even want to do that if I carve up that pretty little face."

Panting, Katalya glanced at the blade and then back toward Mrs. Xiang.

"Do you understand your place now, concubine?"

"I do," replied Katalya, now sobbing.

"Good," replied Mrs. Xiang, directing the servants to release Katalya. A calm returned to Mrs. Xiang. "Then we will have no problems."

"No, Mrs. Xiang."

Mrs. Xiang looked toward one of her servants. "Say good day to Miss Katalya for me."

The air left Katalya's lungs as the large servant slammed his fist into her stomach, causing her to fall to the ground.

"Just remember," said Mrs. Xiang, standing over Katalya, who was gasping for breath. "Your position, right now, lying in the dirt at my feet, is as good as it will ever be for you." She paused and smiled. "You will always be something to be used and cast aside."

Mrs. Xiang stepped over Katalya. "And stay out of my garden," she added as she and her servants walked away, leaving Katalya crying on the ground.

***

Katalya sat at the edge of her bed, awaiting Mr. Xiang's knock on her door. Staring at the

door, she wondered what would happen now.
She knew Xiang was falling for her — at least
enough to ignore traditional household rules
regarding concubines. But now Mrs. Xiang had
made it clear such behavior would be punished.
Now she was faced with the choice of
displeasing her master or infuriating his wife.

She saw a shadow move past the window.
Her stomach tightened with anxiety as she rose
to answer the door.

The door blasted open.

"Get down!" shouted a large, uniformed
man with a rifle.

Katalya let out a scream as she fell to the
floor.

"Shut up!" ordered the man as two more
men entered her house.

The rattle of automatic gunfire caused her
to let out a gasp and tightened her body into a
ball on the floor.

"Clear!" shouted one of the men as he
stepped back into the room from Katalya's
kitchen. "He's not here."

A powerful hand grabbed Katalya's arm,
jerking her to her feet.

She looked into the dark eyes of the man
who had kicked her door open. She had never
seen one before, but she knew they were
Humani soldiers.

"Where the fuck is this guy?" complained another soldier. He was tall, with a thick, well-trimmed black beard.

The man holding Katalya, depressed a button on a communicator on his neck. "Alpha this is Sierra 1-1, Package is not in the small house … just … just a …"

"I am Mr. Xiang's concubine," she said out of habit.

"… just a whore," continued the man.

"Shit," added the bearded soldier. "This dude's living out here in the Dark Zone in this big fucking house and pretty little thing like this." He laughed. "He might as well be a First Family member."

"Watch yourself, Private," said the man holding Katalya, glancing toward another Humani soldier entering the room.

The new soldier glared at the private before turning toward the man holding Katalya.

"I'll deal with him, Sir," said the man holding Katalya.

"Very well, Sergeant Yates," replied the officer, "we need to get back to the rendezvous point."

"And this one?" asked Yates as Katalya felt him give her a shove toward the officer.

"Bring her with us. We're bringing all of the servants to the rendezvous point to …" He paused.

"Yes, Sir," replied Yates. "Let's move, Mr. Xiang's concubine."

Katalya jumped as another burst of automatic gunfire echoes across the estate.

"She's a jumpy one," said the man with the beard.

"Alpha this is Sierra 3, Package in hand," came over the comms circuit.

"Roger 3," replied the officer. He turned toward his men. "Move out!" he ordered, exiting the cottage.

A shove from Yates forced Katalya into movement and she began to walk toward the exit.

"Does she count as a war prize?" asked the man with the beard.

Katalya's gaze shot toward the man. Could that happen?

"No, but you just won an hour of extra duty cleaning weapons," replied Yates. "Act like a soldier and not a fucking merc," he added. "And maybe see who's in the room before you talk shit about the First Families."

Katalya and the three soldiers made their way back to the main estate, the occasional crack and rattle of gunfire punctuating the darkness along the way. As they neared the main entrance to the estate, Katalya saw the glow of the lights at the main entrance. Walking closer, several Humani soldiers came into view standing around a group of servants kneeling in front of the entrance.

"Go kneel over there," ordered Yates, adding one last nudge sending Katalya stumbling forward.

In an attempt to regain her footing, she almost tripped over a body lying in front of her. Glancing at the corpse, she realized it was the body of the servant who had punched her in the stomach earlier.

Quickly turning away, she made her way to the others and knelt beside the head servant, Charles.

"What is happening?" she asked.

"Mr. Xiang's bet on the Red Cloths must have been wrong," replied Charles. "I —"

"Quiet!" ordered a soldier as he pushed Charles to the ground with a boot to his back. "No talking."

Katalya extended her hand to help Charles get back to his knees. As she did, she could see the something in his eyes she had never seen before — fear.

"Charlie Actual, this is Alpha. Package in hand. Request evac," spoke Lieutenant Tacitus into his communicator.

"Roger Alpha. Transports in route," came the reply.

As the report echoed across the yard, Katalya saw Mr. and Mrs. Xiang exit the house.

"Stop!" pleaded Mr. Xiang. "Wait ... we can make a deal."

The solider next to him laughed. "Oh, we're gonna make a deal, guy," he replied, grabbing Xiang's shirt. "You're gonna go up to our little ship and then you're gonna tell us everything you know about the Red Cloths." He released Xiang. "Then we're gonna ship you off to a nice comfy Humani prison."

"I will tell you everything I know ... you don't have to —"

"We don't have to ... but we're going to anyway," replied the solider. "You're gonna be what we call an 'example' to other wannabe lords that think you can challenge Humani interests."

"Please," replied Xiang. "You can take anything you want."

His eyes met Katalya.

"There," he continued. "My concubine ... take her ..."

Katalya turned away, looking toward the ground.

"... she's very —"

"We don't need your permission," laughed the guard. "We could take everything you own ... everything ... and there's nothing you can do about it."

"Please. There is —"

"Be quiet, Cal," interrupted Mrs. Xiang. "Show some dignity."

"At least your wife has some balls," said the soldier.

"Shut up, Humani pig," replied Mrs. Xiang defiantly.

"LT!" shouted the soldier. "Is the wife part of the package?"

"No, just him," replied Tacitus. "We —"

"Good," said the solider and he drew his pistol, placed it against Mrs. Xiang's temple, and fired.

Katalya involuntarily let out a scream.

"Damn it, Private," shouted Tacitus. "Holster that fucking weapon!"

"What does it matter, LT? We're gonna waste all of 'em anyway."

A bolt of shock raced down Katalya's spine and her heart stopped momentarily.

"Private Alama," growled Tacitus, with a glance toward Katalya and the other servants. "You need to ..." He turned toward Yates. "Sergeant Yates, deal with that," he ordered in frustration.

"Yes, Sir," replied Yates as he marched over to Alama and began to whisper in his ear.

"But Sergeant, we have orders to —"

"Attention!" boomed Yates. Alama snapped to attention. "You don't fucking move until the transport gets here."

Turning around Yates' eyes met Katalya's. She felt a chill wash over her body and turned away, closing her eyes and turning her head toward the ground. Her body began to shake as she contemplated what would come next.

"It will be okay, Katalya," whispered Charles and she felt his hand gripping hers. "You will be rewarded for your suffering. In this world or the next."

She looked into his eyes. Although she knew it meant nothing, his words were comforting. She smiled at him.

The roar of a transport drew her attention, but she instantly turned away as the ship's thrusters created a whirlwind of dust and debris. After a moment, the engines began to idle and the dust storm eased.

"Get him onboard!" ordered Tacitus over the hum of the transport's engines.

"You too, Alama," ordered Yates to the private that had killed Mrs. Xiang.

In her periphery, Katalya could see her master — the man who had purchased and used her body — shoved into a Humani transport to be tortured and imprisoned.

"Everyone but Yates load up!" yelled Tacitus.

Still staring at the ground, Katalya heard the other soldiers moving past her as they boarded the transport. Her pulse quickened with each soldier that passed her until it felt as if her heart would explode out of her chest. She closed her eyes and her short, troubled life began to play out in her head.

"They're all onboard," reported Yates to Tacitus.

"Alright, Sergeant," said Tacitus flatly.

"Shitty day, Sir."

"That's why you're handling this and not a jackass like Alama. He would enjoy what is coming next ... and it is nothing to be enjoyed."

"They'll learn, Sir," replied Yates. "Maybe not Alama, but the rest will."

"And I want it done right, Sergeant. One shot. Quick."

Tears began to flow down Katalya's cheeks.

"Yes, Sir," replied Yates as Katalya heard the unmistakable sound of a pistol being pulled from a holster.

Her body began to shake again as she heard footsteps moving toward her.

"I'll start on the left, Sergeant and you can —"

"I'll do it all, LT," interrupted Yates. "You just be ready for runners."

Katalya realized she was panting, unable to bring in air to her lungs.

The hard barrel of Yate's pistol pressed against the back of her head and she let out a gasp, unable to control her sobbing.

"Sorry, girl," said Yates.

She closed her eyes.

"Sergeant Yates!" shouted Tacitus. "Stand down."

The pressure of the pistol against Katalya's head disappeared as Yates holstered the weapon. An uncontrolled groan of anxiety, fear, and despair escaped her lungs.

"Sir?" he asked.

"Just got word from company command … Captain Stone talked to the major and convinced him these people are not a security risk."

"Roger that," replied Yates. "So what do we do with them?"

Katalya's eyes were wide, staring at the ground, as she tried to control her breathing while the two Humani discussed the fate of her and the others as if they were livestock.

"Let them go," ordered Tacitus.

"Get up, girl," ordered Yates as she felt him grab her arm, lifting her to her feet. "All of you, on your feet."

"What will we do?" asked Charles.

"That's not the Guard's problem," replied Tacitus. "Just be glad you're still alive."

Katalya looked toward Yates. The man who was so willingly going to put a bullet in her brain had a clear expression of relief on his face.

"Thank you," said Charles to Tacitus.

"Don't thank us," replied Yates. "Just make the most of what has happened here tonight."

"But what do we do?" asked Katalya without realizing it.

Yates stepped close to her, looking into her eyes. "Live," he said. "Live."

Chapter 10

Katalya groaned as she pulled the water bladder out of the stream. The cold splash of water on her face and neck refreshed her, offering some relief from the mid-afternoon heat. She knelt down, tying off the top of the bladder.

"Sure would be nice to go for a swim," said Dari, pulling another bladder from the water.

"How old are you?"

"Twenty, but that doesn't mean I can't like swimming."

"We've got too much work to do," replied Katalya. "We —"

"Mama!"

Katalya spun around just as her daughter leapt into her arms. "Easy, Sierra," said Katalya. "Mama's working."

"Papa said me and Renny and can go swimming," replied Sierra.

Katalya looked into the green eyes of her eight-year-old daughter and smiled.

She looked so much like her sister, Mori. Or at least what she remembered she looked like.

"But you have to finish your chores after dinner," came a voice from behind Katalya.

Katalya stood and wrapped her arms around Charles, kissing him gently.

"You're too easy on them," she said with a smile, rubbing Sierra's raven hair.

"Yeeaaaahh!" squealed Renny, Sierra's seven-year-old brother as he raced past Katalya and jumped into the stream.

"Mama?" asked Sierra, her green eyes pleading to her mother.

"Go," replied Katalya, feigning exasperation.

"Pushover," said Charles as Sierra leapt into the water.

"Whatever," replied Katalya, hefting the water bladder over her shoulder. "Some of us have work to do."

"I'll walk with you," said Charles.

She turned toward Charles. "Well one of us needs to stay with —"

"I'll do it," interrupted Dari, hefting her bladder onto Charles' shoulder before he could react.

Before Katalya could speak, Dari was in the water.

"I guess that's covered," grunted Charles as he struggled to balance the sudden weight of the bladder.

"Just for a bit," shouted Katalya to Dari. "Then back to —" She stopped, realizing that even if they could hear her over the splashing and the laughter, they would have ignored her. "Lost cause," she huffed, turning toward Charles. "Let's go."

***

"You know they're spoiled," she said as the sound of the children playing faded.

"Yeah ..." acknowledged Charles. "I know."

"So, what do you want to talk about?" she asked. She knew her husband well enough to know he wanted to talk about something.

"Well," said Charles, a smile coming to his face, "The crops have been pretty good the last few years."

"Yes, they have," replied Katalya.

"They've been good enough that Mr. Zu made me an offer on the land."

"That's wonder —" She paused. "You refused, of course?"

98

He remained silent.

Katalya let the bladder fall to the ground with a splash. "You sold our land? I ... Why? This land is what keeps us from ..." She paused, taking a deep breath. "I don't —"

"Whoa," interrupted Charles. "I did it for these," he said, pulling a transportation slip from his pocket.

"What is this?" she asked, snatching the paper from his hand.

She examined the slip:

MARKET CITY TRANSPORT RECIEPT: NUMBER OF PASSENGERS: 5 DESTINATION: PORT ROYAL TRANSFER STATION

She looked up toward Charles.

"We have enough for a transport to Port Royal and from there the agent in town set up passage into Akota territory." He paused, placing his hands on her cheeks. "You're going home, Kat ... with your family."

She couldn't breathe. She looked at the slip again. After all of these years, she held in her hands a piece of paper that represented the freedom she'd thought she would never find. Tears began to roll down her cheeks as she leapt into Charles' arms, knocking his water bladder to the ground. "Thank you ... thank you ... thank you," she repeated, kissing him after each thank you. "When?"

"The flight leaves a week from today," he replied. "And Mr. Zu said we could stay here until we leave for Market City in five days.

"And five passengers?" she asked. "Does that mean Dari —"

"Yes — Dari too. I know she's become like a little sister to you."

"I ... kiss me," she demanded, pulling him to her. She ran her hands over the back of his neck. "It just doesn't feel real."

"It's real, Kat," he replied. "You'll be home in less than two standard months."

"Who else knows?"

"No one yet. I thought we could tell them at dinner tonight."

"Oh," gasped Katalya, still trying to catch her breath. "The workers?"

"Mr. Zu signed an agreement to keep them on at the same wages and with the same housing arrangement for the next four seasons."

"So this is really happening?"

"It's really happening," replied Charles.

She wrapped her arms around him again. Looking down, she noticed what water was left of the water trickling out of the bladders. "The water," she declared.

"Don't worry," said Charles. "You head back to house. I'll refill them ... you have some packing to do."

She exhaled a long breath, unleashing years of anxiety. "Hurry," she said with smile.

***

Katalya sat on the edge of her bed staring at an empty suitcase.

She had started to pack but her heart began to race and she needed to calm herself. In the years since the Humani soldiers took her master, she had experienced happiness unlike any she'd ever thought possible since she was taken from her parents. She'd fallen in love with Charles, had two happy, beautiful children, and her and Charles had managed to take a small part of Xiang's land make a successful farm. But the thought of returning to her native territory had done something the last nine years of peace and happiness had still been unable to achieve — the weight of loss and anxiety had floated away almost instantly.

She let her torso fall back onto the bed. She looked up at the small fan on the ceiling as it slowly rotated. Closing her eyes, she fell into a deep, blissful sleep.

***

The roar of a ship passing overhead startled Katalya from her sleep.

Rising from the bed, she walked toward the main room as the house began to shudder and shake. The ship passed and the house began to settle. She opened the door to look outside. Her pulse quickened as she saw an old military transport stop above the lower field, hovering.

"No," she murmured.

Another ship streaked into position next to the first ship from the opposite direction and both began to descend below the tree line.

"No," she said aloud, walking toward the ships.

A burst of gunfire rattled in the distance.

"No!" she shouted as she burst into a sprint.

Racing toward the sound of gunfire, she saw two farm workers running toward her.

"Slavers!" shouted one of them as they ran past Katalya.

Her heart pounded as she rushed toward her children. Another ship roared past Katalya as she entered the small orchard between the main yard and the upper field.

"No. No. No," she huffed as another burst of gunfire echoed through the orchard. She tried to push her body to go faster, but she couldn't.

Exiting the orchard, she stopped suddenly when she saw two water bladders lying on the ground. "Charles!" she yelled, picking up a large rock next to the bladder.

Katalya's lungs ached and her muscles burned as she crossed the upper field and rushed into the thick brush leading to the lower field. Sliding down the brushy embankment, she jumped back to her feet and burst from the brush into the lower field. Before she could react, she slammed into a tall, thin man wearing worn military clothing and holding a rifle.

"Whoa, missy," said the man, grabbing her arm.

Without thinking, she swung hard, bringing the rock in her hand against the temple of the man. He let out a grunt and fell to the ground.

Pain shot through her left leg as a pistol cracked and she fell to the ground, letting out a cry of agony. Grunting through the pain, she pushed her torso off the ground.

Then everything went black as a boot slammed against her head.

Groaning as she regained consciousness, Katalya slowly opened her eyes. Through her blurred vision, she saw two men standing over her. One was older, his beard peppered with gray, and the other was massive, with a shaved head and muscled arms pressing against the sleeves of his shirt. The older man was holding a pistol.

"You okay, Jax," said the older man.

"My fucking head hurts," cursed the man Katalya had struck as he joined the other two.

"This little bitch fucked you up," laughed the large man.

"She surprised me," retorted Jax. "But I'll make her pay for it," he added, stepping toward her.

"Wait," ordered the older man. "We gotta check her first. If she's a match, you ain't touching her … for anything."

Katalya tried to kick away, only to have the large man grab her injured leg. She cried out as pain raced from her leg throughout her body.

"Don't get squirrely, girl," said the old man as he pulled a small device from his vest. "We just need to check and see if Jax is getting paid or getting laid," he said with a smile.

"I think I'd rather get laid," grumbled Jax, looking down on Katalya. "… teach this bitch some manners," he mumbled.

The older man pressed the device against Katalya's leg. She let out a grunt as a sharp needle punctured her skin. She looked up toward the old man as he held the device to his face.

"Paid it is," declared the old slaver. "Tie her up and stop that bleeding from her leg … they don't pay if she's dead."

Despite the pain radiating through her leg, Katalya kicked at Jax as reached for her.

"Stop kicking," he grunted, slapping Katalya across the face.

The old man stepped forward. "Jax! I fuckin' told you —"

"I ain't leavin' no marks," interrupted Jax. "Just keeping her still," he added as he pulled restraints from his vest.

The restraints pulled tight around Katalya's hands, pressing her wrists together. She felt a sharp prick and looked to see Jax injecting something into her leg.

Almost instantly the pain shifted from pulsating bursts of pain to a dull ache.

"Too bad," said Jax as he applied a coagulant gel to Katalya's wounds. "You look like a wild one."

"Jax, if you can't keep your hands off the goods I'll get —"

"I'm just window shoppin' boss," replied Jax.

As he spoke, Katalya could feel his eyes roaming over her body.

"Well you can look, but don't touch," said the older man. "Let's see if we got any others," he continued, activating a radio on is vest. "Everyone back to the ships."

Katalya was lifted to her feet as Jax jerked on the rope attached to her restraints. "Let's go," he grumbled.

She grunted with each step as she stumbled toward three transports at the far end of the field. Despite the pain, she desperately searched for her children and —.

Katalya fell to her knees, letting out a groan that echoed across the field when she saw Charles' bloody body laying among the plowed rows. "No!" she wailed as Jax jerked on her restraints. But she couldn't move; her muscles refused to react as she sobbed.

"Get up!" shouted Jax, giving another jerk on the ropes.

Her body slid in the dirt but her muscles still failed to respond. All she could do was weep, her body convulsing with each forced breath.

"Just pick her up," said the older slaver.

She panted, unable to bring in enough air as Jax lifted her onto his shoulder. "No!" she moaned as the slavers continued toward the transports. Unable to look away from Charles' body, each step seeming like another kilometer further away from him through tear-fogged vision.

Suddenly a bolt of clarity shot through her. Where were her children?

She tilted her body, looking over Jax's shoulder to see a group of people being herded into a group in front of the transports.

"Sierra!" she screamed as she saw her daughter setting among the workers.

The girl looked up. "Mama!" she yelled as she rose. Before she could get to her, one of the slavers shoved her back to the ground.

Next to Sierra sat Renny and Dari.

Reaching the others, Katalya began to struggle to free herself from Jax grasp.

"There," grumbled Jax as he tossed Katalya onto the ground with the other captives.

She let a groan as her injured leg hit the ground, but her thoughts were on her children. Crawling the few meters to them, she wrapped her restrained arms around them.

"Where's daddy?" asked Renny.

"He got away," said Katalya, lying.

As she looked up, tears filled her eyes as her gaze met Dari's. She could tell Dari knew Charles was dead. "It will be okay," she said, trying to calm her children. "It will be —"

With a powerful jerk, Renny was pulled from Katalya's arms, followed by Sierra.

"No!" she cried, trying to rise to her feet only to be kicked back to the ground. She attempted to push herself up, but she was pinned to the ground by the weight of a man's boot on her back.

"Calm down," said Jax, standing over Katalya. "We just need to see who's going where."

"Let's get this over with and get off this shithole," said a tall man next to Jax. He held a device similar to the one the older man had used on her.

Starting to Katalya's left, the man began to walk down the line of captives. "No," he said after testing the first worker.

"He's in good shape. Port Royal exchange," said the old slaver.

"No," said the tall man after the second.

"Pretty enough," declared the old man. "Recreation market."

Katalya closed her eyes tightly. This could not be happening again.

"No."

"Labor."

Katalya felt the man grab her arm while she was still on the ground.

"This one's going to Navato," said Jax.

She saw the man's boot as he walked past her to the next worker.

"No."

"Too old," said the old slaver.

The crack of a pistol caused Katalya to jerk. She opened her eyes just as the body of Francis Bee, her oldest employee, fell to the ground.

Staring into the vacant eyes of Francis, Katalya's heart began to pound and her breath grew heavy.

"No."

"Labor."

Katalya looked into Dari's eyes again as the tall man read the testing machine after injecting her.

"Yes."

"Navato," replied the old man.

Katalya saw the man grab Renny's arm. He struggled but he was so small, the man almost lifted him into the air as the tested him.

"No."

The old man paused. Looking over Renny. "Too young."

"No!" wailed Katalya as the man placed the pistol to the back of Renny's head.

The pistol cracked and Katalya let out a scream that rolled across the field. Still pressed to the ground by Jax, her tears and saliva formed a coating of mud on her face and around her mouth as she moaned into the dirt. The man grabbed the arm of her crying daughter, Katalya's body began to convulse as she struggled to breathe.

"Yes."

"Navato."

Her mouth filled with mud and gritty earth, Katalya exhaled a long breath of relief as the morbid lottery continued. By the end, the crack of the tall man's pistol no longer phased her. Katalya's yes were dry, unable to cry anymore, as she stared helplessly at Renny's body as the slavers milled around, talking and laughing.

"So five for Navato," said the old man. "Better than average." He turned toward the tall man. "The Navatos go to my transport."

Katalya felt her body lifted off the ground.

"Let's go pretty," said Jax with a smile.

Katalya had nothing left. She stared vacantly at him.

"Let's go," ordered the old man as he stopped beside Jax and Katalya. "And keep this one away from her daughter. Never keep the families together," he warned. "The fathers get heroic and the mothers ..." The old man placed his hand on Katalya's jaw, forcing him to look into his eyes. "... you have no idea what they'll do. I learned that the hard way." He moved closer to her. "But it really is a shame you're a Navato; you'd be a fun ride."

Katalya looked up toward the man. Her heart stopped as a she looked into the eyes of the source of so many of her nightmares.

"You're the boss, Tamar," replied Jax.

Katalya leaped toward the man. Trying to use the only weapon available against the man who had repeatedly raped her mother, she sank her teeth into his arm.

She bit down hard but her teeth could not penetrate his thick shirt.

The man laughed as he pushed her to the ground. "See what I mean. Get them loaded up."

Katalya looked up the man that ravaged her family. He had no idea who she was. She wondered how many families he had torn apart over the years.

"I'm going to kill you for what you've done," she shouted as Jax pulled her to her feet.

Tamar stopped and turned back toward Katalya.

"Honey, you're not the first crying mother to tell me that, but here I am, still livin'. I've done far worse than what's happened here today and I'm sure someday someone will get their revenge on me, but it will be some Terillian Ranger or maybe a merc, not some weeping mother — even a pretty one like you," he added with a smile. Tamar turned toward the tall man. "Load the rest in the other two transports and head for the market. These five plus the others is enough for a delivery. I'll leave for Navato. You guys stay in Port Royal until I get back." He paused. "And tell the boys the money from the normal ones is there's to split per their contracts."

"You got it," replied the tall man with a smile. "They'll be happy to hear it."

"Just keep them from getting themselves killed in any bar fights until I get back," replied Tamar before he turned to Jax. "Now let's get our cargo onboard."

Chapter 11

"Kat," said Dari, shaking Katalya's shoulder. "You need to eat."

Katalya lay motionless on the floor — just like she had for the last two days. In the span of less than an hour she had gone from being on the verge of returning to her native land to having her husband and son killed while both she and her daughter had become slaves. Unable to see her daughter, she had cried nonstop for the first day. After that, her emotions were sapped; she had nothing left to feel but pain.

And it consumed her. Unable to even draw the strength to eat, she simply lay on the floor, like the thing she had once again become.

"Katalya," repeated Dari. "You have to eat."

Katalya heard Dari; she just couldn't move.

"You're not a quitter," said Dari. "We're not quitters. What would your mother have done?"

Katalya was instantly on her knees, gripping Dari's shirt with her fists and shoving her onto the cold hard deck of their cell. "My mother!" she growled. "My mother gave everything … everything to keep me alive and out of …" She paused as the tears she had been unable to cry for days began to flow again. "And look what good it did. I'm here again. It was for nothing, all of it for nothing. Charles is dead …" She paused again. "Renny … There's no —"

Katalya tumbled backwards as Dari pushed her off of her and onto the deck. "Shut up!" she growled. "Your mother was a fighter. I have listened to you talk about her for years. She may not have been a soldier but she was just as brave and sacrificed just as much."

"For what?"

"For what?" retorted Dari. "For the life you still have. Your heart's still beating … and don't you forget, so is Sierra's … a life that you made. You had nine years most slaves will never experience."

"And it's gone."

"No, it's not … it's still somewhere on this ship. And if you let yourself die … she will have no one to look for her, find her, and save her." Dari paused. Now tears began to form in her own eyes. "My parents sold me for a transport ticket ... yours gave everything for you." She placed her hands on Katalya's cheeks. "What kind of parent do you want to be?"

Dari released her hold on Katalya and moved back to the opposite side of the cell.

Katalya slowly pushed herself into a seated position and picked up the small bowl of food in front of her. Taking the bowl in her hands, she stared at the mixture of rice and vegetables. Her mind drifted and she wondered if her mother was somewhere out there thinking about her right now. She knew if she was still alive, she would be. She took a deep breath and began to eat. The food held no taste, but she ate it.

As she ate, she felt eyes on her. Looking up, she saw Jax standing at the edge of the cell that held her and Dari.

"So, you are alive," said Jax.

Katalya looked back toward her food and returned to her meal.

"Such a waste," continued Jax.

Katalya ignored him.

"I bet you wouldn't be such a bitch if I told you I could let you see your kid," said Jax.

Katalya looked up from her food.

"And I can, you know," he added. "If you play nice."

Dari slid in front of Katalya. "Your boss said you couldn't do anything —"

"Shut up," ordered Jax without looking at Dari. "Do you want to see your girl?" he asked Katalya.

"Yes!" she pleaded.

"Then we will have to come to an agreement."

"Don't," whispered Dari. "He —"

"I want to see her," interrupted Katalya, pushing Dari out of the way.

"Good," said Jax as he opened the cell door and stepped inside. "Then we have an agreement."

"Kat," pleaded Dari.

"You will let me see her?"

Jax nodded. "If you're nice to me … and don't tell Tamar."

"Kat he's —"

"Yes," blurted Katalya.

Jax walked up to Katalya and Dari. "Get to the other side of the cell," he said to Dari.

Dari stared up at him defiantly.

"Go," said Katalya.

"But he's —"

"Go," she said again, adding a slight shove.

Dari reluctantly scooted to the opposite corner of the cell.

"I'll get to see her?" asked Katalya again.

"On your hands and knees," ordered Jax as he undid his belt.

Katalya turned away from Jax and positioned herself in front of him.

"And you, girl with the messed up face. You watch."

"No," replied Dari.

Jax grabbed Katalya's hair, pulling hard so that she was looking at him.

"No deal if she doesn't watch," demanded Jax, as saliva began to pool on the side of his mouth.

Katalya turned slightly toward Dari, pleading with her eyes.

Dari turned, placing her back against the wall so she was facing Katalya and Jax.

She sat motionless.

"See," said Jax, "that wasn't so hard."

Jax's hands gripped Katalya's waist. She turned her head toward the floor and closed her eyes.

She felt the skirt of her dress flip up and his rough fingers grabbing at her undergarment, pulling hard.

Katalya gritted her teeth and let out a grunt and he drove himself into her and began the thrust wildly. After a few rough thrusts, she began to feel him spasm and convulse.

She clinched her jaw forcefully as he let out a loud moan.

As he stood, Katalya rose to her feet and adjusted her clothing. "Let me see her."

"Maybe," said Jax as he wiped drool from his mouth. "If you keep playing nice."

She stared at him wishing she had the ability to kill him. But she knew there was nothing she could do but wait to see if he would follow through.

"I will," she replied. What else could she do?

Jax grabbed her pulling her close, grabbing her breast.

"I guess Tamar was right about one thing," said Jax with a smile. "Who knows what a mother will do for their children."

He slid his hand down her body and under her dress.

She closed her eyes, exhaling hard as he found her.

"I guess we'll just see how much you will do," he said, the alcohol from his breath filling her nostrils.

"Just let me see her," she pleaded.

"Tonight," he replied as he removed his hand from under her dress. Jax looked over toward Dari. "Enjoy the show."

"You will pay for what you've done," said Dari in a low voice.

Jax laughed and turned back toward Katalya. "Remember … you play nice and you see your girl," he added as he turned and exited the cell.

Katalya waited until Jax was out of sight and collapsed onto the floor, sobbing. As she sat on the floor, she felt Dari wrap her arm around her.

"He will pay, Kat."

Unable to speak, Katalya rest her head on Dari's shoulder.

***

"Mama!"

Katalya jumped from her sleep and looked toward the front of the cell.

Standing at the entrance was Jax with Sierra next to him.

"Sierra!" she cried as she rushed toward the bars.

Reaching the bars, she ran her hands over Sierra's arms and then over her hair to her cheeks. "Are you okay, baby?"

"I want to be with you, Mommy," she said, her eyes red with tears and her body shaking with fear.

"I know, baby. And I want to be with you. Just do what they say and know that I love you."

"Okay, that's it," said Jax as he picked up Sierra.

"Mama!" she yelled.

"Tell her to be quiet," warned Jax, "or you'll never see her again."

"Sweetie, be quiet," pleaded Katalya. "I will see you again."

She looked toward Jax, her eyes begging him.

"Yes, little one," he said, looking over Katalya's body. "If your mommy is nice to Uncle Jax, you will see her again."

"I will be," begged Katalya.

"Now cover your ears," said Jax to Sierra as he set her back on the deck. "I need to tell your mommy a secret."

"Do it, baby," added Katalya.

As Sierra placed her hands on her ears, Jax leaned in too close to Katalya, running his rough hand over hers. "I am going to do things to you that you never thought a man could do to a woman," he said with sick smile. "And if you let me do it without saying a word to Tamar, I'll let you see her every night after we play."

"I understand," she replied with a glance toward her daughter.

"I want you to say that I can do whatever I want to you."

She looked into his eyes with a combination of desperation and hatred. "You can do whatever you want to me."

"I hope hitting me with that rock was worth it," said Jax, "because I want you to think about that every time you feel me inside you." He paused, running his hand over Sierra's head as she held her hands over her ears. "Tell me you want me."

"I want you," she replied.

"Then you better show it," he replied as he gently moved Sierra's hands from her ears. "Mommy and Uncle Jax are done talking," he said gently. "Now say goodbye to Mommy."

"Mommy?"

"It's okay, baby," she replied, tears now streaming down her cheeks. "I'll see you soon."

"When do you want to see her?" asked Jax.

"Tomorrow," begged Katalya. "Tomorrow."

"Then I'll see you tomorrow," replied Jax with a content smile. "Now let's get you back to bed," he said, turning toward Sierra. "Your mommy's gonna need her rest for tomorrow."

Chapter 12

Katalya gripped the bars of her cell and closed her eyes as Jax let out a guttural groan. As he stepped away, she released the bars and turned toward him. Over the last three weeks, Jax had made true on his promise — by letting her see Sierra daily and playing out his depraved fantasies with her every night.

"Can I see her tomorrow?" asked Katalya. He always made her ask after.

"Sorry," replied Jax. "But you won't be able to see her anymore."

Katalya's heart fell. "Why? What happened to her?"

"She fine," said Jax. "Just has a different destination than you. We're coming out of our jump and docking in a few hours."

Katalya stepped toward Jax, grabbing his still-unbuttoned shirt. "Don't take her away from me … leave her with me … or send me with her." Tears welled in her eyes as she begged him. "She's all I have left."

Jax pushed Katalya away.

"She's not yours anymore," he replied. "The little ones are being transferred for a ship bound for Capro and the adults go to Navato."

Katalya had never heard of either place. "Why can't we go together?"

"I don't fucking know. I just know what I get paid for."

"You can't," she pleaded, grabbing his arms. "You promised to —"

Jax slammed her against the wall, taking her breath.

"I promised to let you see your pup if you played along."

As he spoke, Katalya felt his body pressing against hers.

"But just because she's gone, doesn't mean we can't make another agreement," he added, running his hand down her back.

"Get off of me!" she grunted, twisting her body away from him.

Jax grabbed her again, slamming her back against the bars. She turned her head as he raised his hand.

But the blow did not come and she opened her eyes.

"If only I could," mumbled Jax. "Tamar wants you all free of bumps and bruises."

"Then you need to keep your hands off me," she whispered.

The pressure on Katalya's arms increased as Jax squeezed her arms tightly.

"Don't worry, you little Dark Zone trash," he smiled. "You won't be the last. And besides …" He paused as he looked over her body, "… I have a good memory, so I'll be thinking about you for a long time," he added with a smile. "Long after the Humani have done what they want with your little brat and the lizards are done with you."

Jax leaned in, running his tongue over Katalya's cheek. "Maybe you'll look back on our time together and wish you could have it this good again."

She curled her body away from him and walked to the far corner of her cell.

"If you change your mind, let me know," said Jax before he turned and walked out of her cell.

Katalya sat in the corner of her cell, her knees pulled to her forehead.

Hopelessness consumed her.

"I'm sorry," said Dari. "I —"

"You're sorry," snapped Katalya. "Remember when you said that I had to fight for my girl. Well I did …" She looked up toward

Dari. "I let that … that pig do those things to me. And what happened? She's still gone."

"You saw her every day for three weeks," replied Dari. "It was only a few minutes but those are minutes you wouldn't have had —"

"How can you be so fucking —," Katalya let out a grunt of frustration. "I have nothing left to live for."

Dari placed her hand on Katalya's shoulder. "If you give up … then they win," she said softly.

"They've already won," replied Katalya, lowering her head to her knees again.

***

Katalya sank into a fog of despair.

She spent the next week huddled in the corner of her cell, devoid of anything but the constant ache of loss. Throughout each day, she transitioned through an agonizing cycle of silent despair, sudden bursts of tears, and a few, short spells of exhausted sleep punctuated by nightmares.

Dari had been able to get her to drink and occasionally eat, at times spoon feeding her, but it didn't matter to Katalya — nothing mattered. Her stomach ached from hunger and her muscles spasmed from dehydration, but those pains paled in comparison to the searing torment of emptiness in her heart which burned like a knife constantly twisting and digging into her soul.

"Just one more bite," said Dari, placing the spoon against Katalya's lips.

Katalya sensed the pressure and slowly opened her mouth, allowing Dari to feed her. Mechanically chewing her food, she could hear Dari speak.

"You need to get your strength up. I've heard them say we are pulling into Navato tomorrow, wherever that is."

Katalya continued chewing her food.

"I heard them mention the Xen," continued Dari. "I didn't even think they existed. I mean, lizard men? And why did they pick us?"

"It doesn't matter," replied Katalya. "We're all going to die."

"We don't know what's going to happen."

Katalya stopped chewing and looking into Dari's eyes. "You're right. Maybe they won't kill us. Maybe they'll just beat us, or make us work in mines until we die, or maybe just rape us every day."

Dari placed her hand on Katalya's shoulder. "Just one more bite."

Katalya opened her mouth as Dari gave her another spoonful.

"They'll pay someday," mumbled Dari as Katalya stared into the distance.

✱✱✱

Katalya awoke with Jax on top of her.

"Shhh …" warned Jax, glancing toward the sleeping Dari as he slid his hand up Katalya's leg.

She looked back at him with vacant eyes as he pushed her dress up to her waist.

"You're too good to not get just one more taste," he whispered, positioning himself between her legs. "One last time before you get handed over to the lizards."

She heard him undoing his belt but lay motionless, staring at the gray ceiling.

He let out a groan as he pushed inside her.

"I actually think I'm gonna miss y —"

From her back, Katalya saw Dari grab Jax's hair and pull his head back. As she did, Dari drove the handle of her spoon into Jax's right eye.

Jax let out a scream as he fell backwards, the spoon still protruding from his eyes.

The piercing sound of the scream awoke Katalya from her comatose state. Rage flowed through her as she jumped on top of her attacker. She pulled the spoon from his eyes as Dari struggled to hold his arms.

"Fucking bitches!" shouted Jax. "Help! Help!" he continued as he slammed Dari onto the floor.

Katalya pressed against Jax's forehead as she drove the bloody spoon downward,

126

embedding it in his other eye. Another scream echoed through the cell as Jax released Dari and sent Katalya flying off of him.

Jax pushed himself to his feet and stumbled backwards as he pulled a knife from his belt. He waved the knife wildly as he backpedaled, his face covered in blood. "Help!" he shouted again.

Unable to gain his bearings, Jax slammed into the wall. Jarred by the impact, he dropped the knife. Dari rushed Jax but when she grabbed him, he sensed her and sent her sliding across the floor with a blow to her face.

Seeing the knife hit the floor, Katalya grabbed it from the floor and, as Dari fell backwards past her, stepped forward and drove the blade into Jax's rib cage with a roar of hatred and rage. Jax let out a gasp and Katalya felt his body tighten.

Pushing him onto the floor, she pulled the knife from his chest. Blood sprayed over the floor and her arm and continued to pump from the wound with each beat of his heart. She raised the blade above her head. "Die!" she growled as she drove the knife into his chest again. Closing her eyes, she began to repetitively stab him, letting out a grunt with each thrust as she remembered every time he had penetrated her.

A bolt of electricity shot through her body and everything went black.

Moaning as she regained consciousness, Katalya felt the sting of a shock-dart on her back. Slowly opening her eyes, she saw the bloody body of Jax on the floor next to her. She tried to push herself to her feet, but the weight of a boot drove her back to the floor.

She looked up toward Tamar.

"Hold still," he said.

"Man, they fucked him up," said another slaver.

Katalya glanced over to see Dari still unconscious on the deck.

"I warned him," replied Tamar. "I keep telling you guys … it's better to just keep it in your pants with the cargo and just get a rec girl or some drunk whore in a bar." He glanced down at Jax's body. His face was covered in blood and his torso was a ragged mess of blood and torn flesh. "Less likely that shit like this will happen."

"You don't have to tell me, boss," replied the slaver as he drew his pistol and pointed it toward Dari's unconscious body.

"No!" shouted Katalya, struggling in vain to free herself from the weight of Tamar's body.

"Wait," ordered Tamar. "Even if they killed Jax, they're still worth 10,000 Humani each … I can replace that bag of meat over there."

The slaver slowly holstered his weapon. "What are we gonna do with him?"

"He'll go out with the trash before we enter the asteroid field," replied Tamar, releasing the pressure on Katalya's back and stepping toward the cell door. "And get this mess cleaned up, including the girl. She's covered in blood," he added before walking away.

Chapter 13

Katalya and Dari watched from their cell as other captives were shuffled past. As another group moved along, she noticed a large, dark-skinned man that stood head and shoulders above the rest. Bound at his wrists, the man's biceps stretched his thin shirt. His hair was cut short, almost like the Humani soldiers she had seen so many years ago.

Their eyes met. She saw a look of determination and defiance burning in his eyes.

"Move!" shouted one of the guards, shoving the man.

The shove failed to move the massive man and he turned toward the guard.

"We'll fucking shock you again," warned another guard as he stepped away from the man, his dart gun at the ready.

The man started to move but the guard shoved him again.

The man spun around, swiftly knocking the weapon from the guard's hands and landing a powerful blow to his jaw. The other guard fired his dart gun into the man's back as the first guard fell to the ground unconscious.

Letting out an angry grunt when the electrical dart sent a powerful shock through his body, the man advanced on the second guard. The same type of dart had knocked Katalya unconscious, but she watched as the man absorbed the bolt of electricity and charged the second guard while he was chambering another dart. Before the guard could bring the weapon to bear, the man knocked the rifle from his hand and in one motion lifted him into the air and slammed him onto the floor with a thud.

He rose to his feet but three more darts tore into his chest.

Overwhelmed, he spasmed and fell to his knees before collapsing to the floor.

"Who is that?" asked Dari.

"I don't know," replied Katalya, watching more guards surround the man.

"He looks like a soldier," said Dari.

"And fights like one," added Katalya.

"I told you sons-of-bitches to bind him tightly," grumbled Tamar as he walked up to the guards struggling to restrain the man. "Maybe we should have just put a bullet in this one," said Tamar, as his men finally restrained the man. "You're almost more trouble than you're worth … literally," declared the old slaver. "You've cost me two …" He paused, looking at the slaver the man had slammed onto the floor. "… probably three men."

"Take these bindings off and I'll kill some more," said the man with a smile as three guards pulled him to his knees.

"So full of defiance," replied Tamar, with a smile of his own. "You should have joined us when you had the chance." Tamar pivoted and slammed his fist into the man's jaw, sending him back to the floor. "But you're too fucking good for that … the reptiles will fix that." He looked toward another slaver standing next to him. "Get him out of here …"

As four guards dragged the massive man away, Tamar looked around the passageway before his gaze landed on Katalya and Dari. "And with these two killing Jax … hell, between them and that bull-headed son-of-a-bitch, my overhead has been cut down by four shares," he added with a laugh. "More credits for old Tamar."

Tamar waved his hand and two slavers approached Katalya's cell.

"Hands through the hole," ordered the slaver.

Katalya extended her hands through the bars and felt the cold metal tighten around her wrists as the slaver applied the bindings.

"You too," he said to Dari.

She also complied and the two were pulled from their cell and hustled toward the transport's hangar bay.

As she entered the hangar, Katalya saw dozens of captives herded into two groups. Just inside the entrance stood a large man. "One!" he shouted and gave a captive a shove to the right. "Two." And another was shoved to the left.

"What are they doing?" asked Dari.

"I don't ..." replied Katalya. "I ..." Katalya stopped as she noticed that Dari had dropped behind her.

"Two!" boomed the large slaver, sending Katalya stumbling to her left.

She turned to see another woman behind her instead of Dari.

"One!" And the woman was moved to the right.

Then she saw Dari.

"Two!"

Dari stepped into line behind Katalya.

"Gotta stay together," whispered Dari.

"Keep moving," ordered another guard.

Katalya turned toward the exit. Ahead of her she saw the large captive that had beaten the two guards in the hangar. He towered over the crowd.

"Count's done," shouted the man at the entrance. "Ninety-six!"

"Hook 'em up!" shouted Tamar from the front of the line.

Katalya was spun to her left as a slaver grabbed her wrists. "Don't move," he ordered as he ran a metal rope through an opening in her bindings. She watched as the same rope was run through the bindings of the other captives in her group.

"When these doors open," continued Tamar, "just keep moving and do as you are told."

Tamar held his hand in the air, moving it in a circular motion. As he did, the exterior doors of the hangar rolled open with a series of metallic screeches and clangs.

Katalya closed her eyes as the hangar filled with a bright light from the exterior of the transport. A sudden jerk on her bindings forced her to move toward the light. Shuffling along with the others, Katalya slowly adjusted to the brightness of the room. Her senses were almost overwhelmed with the scene around her.

The hot, humid air weighed on Katalya's skin like a coat. The sound of machinery and engines echoed through her ears, punctuated by the random orders being shouted by the slavers as the captives continued to move forward. In the background and above her, she could hear strange clicking and hissing sounds. Squinting, the forms on the platforms above her slowly became clear.

Katalya's heart jumped as she saw the creatures. They were short, with brown, scaly skin and elongated snouts protruding from their flat heads. They wore uniforms of green and black tunics with metallic skirts. Some carried short rifles while others, also wearing gold medallions around their short necks, had sidearms and swords attached to their waist belts.

"They must be Xen," said Dari. "They are real."

Katalya couldn't answer; her brain was still processing the creatures in front of her. She watched as they moved along the platform gathering in twos and threes, their long, thin fingers pointing toward her and the other captives as clicks and hisses came from their mouths.

The pressure of metal against her head caused Katalya to look toward the guard in front of her.

"Hold still," he ordered, holding a small piece of metal behind her ear.

She let out a grunt as metallic anchors shot from the small device and embedded into her skin. A loud, high pitched tone rang through her head, causing her to gasp from the pain. She closed her eyes.

Opening her eyes, she looked up toward the creatures.

"Good stock," said one of the creatures wearing a medallion.

Katalya put her hand to the device behind her ear. She could now understand the Xen.

"And these will get the lupus gene treatment?" asked another.

"Yes, Lord Vlara," replied a third, clearly subordinate to the others. "And one is a lineage match with a vulpes sample."

"Excellent," replied first Xen. "We shall test the strength of the strain tomorrow. Do not start the treatment on the new sample until the test is completed."

"I will inform the technicians, Lord Vlara."

Another tug on the line forced Katalya to move again.

The group passed from the open brightness of the massive processing area into the gray, ambient lighting of a large passageway. Once inside, they continued to move down the corridor, with slavers in front, to the side, and in the rear. Even inside, the heat and humidity hung heavy.

They walked past a series of closed doors with markings Katalya had never seen as well as several rooms with windows offering views of what appeared to laboratories. On the other side of the windows were a combination of humans and Xen, busily carrying out various tasks.

"Keep moving," ordered a guard and Katalya and the others received another tug on their bindings.

The group continued through the facility for several moments before abruptly stopping.

Katalya watched as the first few captives were removed from the cable and disappeared into a room. The group began moving again only to stop for more captives to be removed. The next time they stopped, a guard grabbed Katalya's wrists.

"Your turn," he said, removing the cable and her bindings while holding her arm tightly.

She winced as the guard placed a device on her hand, sending a bolt of pain through her body. Holding her hand to her face, she read the text that had been imprinted into her skin.

L-B01-S:A7 0807

"That's your new name … and this is your new home," said the guard.

Katalya looked into the room.

Inside were five small beds, a water fountain, and a partitioned toilet. It was clean, almost sterile. At first glance, it looked better than the many places she had stayed.

"Move," ordered the guard, pressing the barrel of a rifle into Katalya's spine.

She stepped inside the room and was joined by Dari.

"This isn't too bad," said Dari, looking around the room.

The windowless door slammed shut and Katalya turned to see three more captives — a woman and two men. The woman, probably in her early thirties, was tall and thin with long brown hair. The first man was more of a boy. Maybe eighteen standard years old, he was pale and sickly looking. His oversized clothing accentuated his frail build.

The second man was well-muscled and stood well over two meters. Katalya instantly recognized him as the fighter from the hangar bay. He stepped toward Dari and Katalya.

"I am Magnus," he said in a low, powerful voice.

"I'm Dari ... and this is Katalya."

Magnus gave a nod in acknowledgement.

"What are your names?" asked Dari to the others.

"I'm Sariana," said the tall woman.

"I'm Harold Vincent," said the young man. "Does anyone know what we're here for?"

"I don't know," replied Dari. "Something about our blood or something, I think."

"It's a breeding program," said the tall woman. "They've brought us here to be pets in a zoo."

"I don't know … and it doesn't matter," added Magnus. "We need to resist and find a way to escape or die trying."

"We're not warriors," replied Harold. "I'm just a postage sorter. I went to the city for a few drinks and next thing I know I'm on a ship in a cage."

"You don't have a choice," replied Magnus, his dark eyes burning with defiance. "Even if they kill us, we can't just allow them to —"

"Or we can do what we're told and survive," replied Katalya. "Survival as a slave is better than the freedom of death."

Magnus stepped toward Katalya, causing her to back away. His powerful hands wrapped around her arms, holding her gently. She hadn't been held that way since her father. She looked up into his fierce eyes.

"Once you think that way, you are already dead," he said softly. "You were meant to be free, as are all of us. Captivity may have put out the fire in your soul, but the ember is still there."

Katalya felt her stomach tighten as he pressed his hand gently on her stomach.

"I know you can feel it … in your gut."

Her mind told her to step away, but her body failed to respond.

"Close your eyes," he said.

Without thinking, she closed her eyes.

"Think back to a time when you were so free it felt like your heart would fly away."

Katalya's subconscious flashed to a memory of her chasing her sister, Mori, through the fields of her home planet, Pheta. The brisk wind washed across her face and the smell of wildflowers filled her nose as she felt the soft cushion of the grass on her feet.

She opened her eyes and looked into his as tears flowed down her cheeks.

"That is it," Magnus said with a smile. "Freedom. Do you feel it now?"

"Yes," she whispered.

"Now let the ember continue to grow stronger until it is a raging fire. Don't let anyone take that away from you."

"But how —"

"Resist," he replied.

Chapter 14

"807!" shouted the guard through the intercom. "Come to the door!"

Katalya looked at the others.

"You ... black hair, green eyes ... come to the fucking door."

Katalya glanced at Dari and then Magnus. They had only been in the cell a few hours but everyone new Magnus was the leader.

He gave her a nod and she walked to the door.

"Everyone back," ordered the guard, swinging his rifle in the direction of Magnus with one hand and opening the door with the other.

Katalya stepped into the passageway and the guard slammed the door shut.

"Move," he said, giving her a nudge with the barrel of his rifle.

"Where are we —"

Katalya's question was cut short with another rough jab from the rifle's barrel.

"Move," repeated the guard.

Katalya obeyed and began to walk quietly down the maze of corridors and passageways with the guard close behind. They would pass an occasional guard or technician along the way but there were no Xen. As she made her journey down the passageway, she couldn't help but think about what Magnus had said to her earlier.

"Here," said the guard, stopping at a set of double doors to Katalya's right.

Above the doors was a placard with symbols Katalya did not understand over the words TEST ROOM 73C written in the trade language. The doors opened and Katalya stepped inside.

She looked down a long hallway that opened into an empty, oval room.

"Keep moving," said the guard.

Katalya crept toward the opening.

Stepping into the open space, she looked up to see several Xen on the level above her looking down through transparent partitions.

A metallic *clang* caused her to spin around just as a door slid shut, blocking the hallway she had just exited.

She turned back toward the center of the room. Glancing up toward the observers, her heart began to race as she wondered what was going to happen.

"BRING IN SUBJECT V-B12-S:C10 555," blasted over the room's intercom.

Katalya's attention instantly shifted to a door opposite her as it began to slide open. Her heart skipped when it opened to reveal another person.

The woman across from her was tall and thin. Her long, black hair had auburn highlights and fell to her waist. She was looking toward the floor, her hair covering most of her face. Her clothes were similar to the ones Katalya had been given just prior to arrival at the facility, except the woman's was a dull red compared to Katalya's gray pants and shirt. What was visible with the sleeveless shirt was the woman's muscular arms.

"This will be an excellent test of the behavioral element of the serum," Katalya overheard one of the Xen above her say. "The subject has already killed twice on command … but this should be a definitive test of the serum's strength."

Staring at the woman across the room, Katalya saw a flash of the woman's ear; it was pointed at the end and much thinner than normal.

"555!" blasted over the intercom.

The woman looked up and Katalya's heart stopped.

Despite the changes in her hair, the muscular build, and the strange ears, the green eyes were still the same. "Mother?" she gasped.

The woman looked toward Katalya and their eyes met.

"Attack!" blasted over the intercom and the woman exploded into a sprint toward Katalya.

"Mother!" she yelled as she stumbled backwards into the wall.

In a flash, the woman was on her. The air left Katalya's lungs as the woman slammed into her chest, knocking her to the floor. Dazed, Katalya felt the weight of the woman on top of her and looked up to see a row of sharp canine teeth protruding from the woman's mouth.

"Please," begged Katalya. "Mother ... Ina!" she shouted using the Akota language she hadn't spoken in years. "It's me, Katalya ... Kimimila!" she added using her own Akota name.

The teeth sank back into the woman's mouth as she stared down at Katalya. "K ... Kimimila?"

"Ina," she exhaled.

"No," stammered the woman, falling backwards off of Katalya. "No. It can't be."

"It's me," replied Katalya.

"Attack!" blasted the order again.

Sierra shook her head violently. "No!" she shouted. "Not her!"

"Ina?"

Her mother, still shaking her head, grabbed Katalya's arms tightly. "You can't be here ... not you too." Her mother's grip tightened. "Don't let them —"

"Attack!" echoed through the room and again Sierra shook her head as if trying to shake the order from her consciousness. She pulled Katalya close.

"I love you," she said, almost pleading. "Fight them," she whispered as her canines began to recede again. "Don't become —"

"Attack!"

Sierra stumbled backwards, away from Katalya. "No!" growled Sierra as she turned and leapt toward the Xen in the upper level.

Leaping almost her height, Sierra grabbed a bracket holding the transparent partition and began to pull herself over the barrier. A Xen in a military uniform stepped forward and struck Sierra with the butt of a rifle, sending her falling to the floor as an alarm began to blare and the words "SECURITY ALERT" blasted over the intercom.

"Mother!" shouted Katalya as the opposite door slid open and two guards rushed in.

Sierra paused. Her gaze burned into Katalya's heart. "I love you," she said before turning toward the guards as they ran into the room.

The guards attempted to bring their weapons to bear but Sierra was too fast. Leaping into the air, Sierra landed on the torso of the first guard and sank her teeth into his neck. The man let out an ear-piercing scream as Sierra jerked her head back, taking a chunk out of the man's throat. Blood flowed from his neck as he fell to the ground. She turned toward the next guard.

A shot echoed through the room as Sierra crumpled to the ground.

"No!" screamed Katalya, falling to her knees.

"Fucking rabid dog," cursed the second guard, still holding his pistol on Sierra's motionless body.

Rage enveloped Katalya as her vision tunneled and she rushed toward the guard.

A blow to her temple from the side of the guard's pistol sent her reeling backwards. Dazed, she rushed him again only to be knocked to the ground with a right hand. "Crazy bitch," laughed the guard. "You don't have the juice for that yet … and you definitely don't have the teeth."

She pushed herself off the floor but staggered, still stunned from the blow.

"Remove the subjects," came across the announcing circuit. "Destroy V serum, subject 555."

"No!" moaned Katalya as she rushed toward her mother and fell to her knees beside Sierra's lifeless body. Taking her mother in her arms, she began to rock back and forth. "No. No. No," she repeated.

"Get up!" came a voice from behind her as she was ripped from her mother.

"No!" she screeched as two guards began to drag her back to the hallway. She kicked and shook her body, but they were too strong to resist. As she struggled, she looked up, letting out a primal groan as she saw another guard dragging her mother away by one of her feet, like an animal.

Her body went limp.

Sobbing, she closed her eyes as the guards returned her to her cell.

***

Her face red with tears, Katalya stepped into the cell.

She saw the shocked look on the faces of Dari, Sariana, and Harold.

"What happened?" asked Dari, placing her hand on Katalya's shoulder.

Katalya's gaze shifted to Magnus, who was standing behind the others. With a blank glance toward Dari, she walked over the Magnus. "Can you teach me how to kill them?" she asked.

Chapter 15

An exhausted Katalya stood in front of yet another lab tech.

Sleep eluded her. The vision of her mother being killed flashed like an explosion in her mind almost every time she closed her eyes. When sleep finally came, she relived the scene again, only with her being the monster and her own daughter being across from her.

But things were different. Unlike when she was taken before, rage had replaced despair and despite her exhaustion, she stared defiantly into the eyes of the technician standing in front of her in the laboratory.

"Just hold still," said the frail-looking lab tech as he grabbed her hand and extended it outward. "Just a little —"

Katalya jerked her arm away, still staring into the tech's eyes.

"Guard!" shouted the tech.

A blow to the back of her head dazed Katalya.

"Do as you're told, cow," ordered the guard.

She turned toward the guard. "Fuck you."

Another blow almost knocked her to the ground. She turned back toward the guard, ready for her beating.

"You just don't know when to stop," he replied, raising his hand.

Out of the corner of her eye she saw Magnus, who was at another station. He shook his head, suggesting to Katalya that now was not the time. She slowly turned back toward the tech and extended her arm.

"That's a good cow," said the guard.

Returning her gaze toward the tech, she gritted her teeth as he injected something into her arm and turned toward a data recorder next to her. "First injection for L-B01-S:A7 0807," he spoke into the recorder.

She involuntarily rubbed her arm. The injection site began to burn.

"Move on," said the tech with a glance toward the guard.

Hiding the pain that was now pulsing through her arm with each beat of her heart, Katalya stepped away from the station and joined the others in a temporary holding cell in the lab.

"It hurts," said Dari.

"I fear it will get worse," replied Magnus, rubbing his forearm.

"When can we fight them?" asked Katalya, grimacing from the growing pain. "You said we need to resist."

"Yes," replied Magnus, "but we must know what we are fighting. We observe as much as we can and learn about their routines and then we have a chance at not only killing some of them but maybe escaping."

"Then why did you attack those guards on the transport?" asked Katalya, the need for revenge burning at her soul.

"Because I knew we were leaving the ship and I had nothing to lose." He looked toward Katalya and smiled. "And besides, my little warrior, you don't even know how to fight yet."

Her body grew hot. He had preached defiance but now talked of patience? "You —" She paused as her skin began to burn and her head spun. She looked over to see Dari stumble into Magnus' arms.

"It burns," said Dari.

Katalya's vision began to blur and everything went dark.

***

Katalya awoke to the sound of her own screams, pain radiating from her burning skin. Her muscles spasmed and she let out another cry of agony. Curling her body into a ball, she began to pant as she struggled to bring in enough air with each labored breath. Through her clouded vision she looked across the room to see Dari rolling on the floor with her hands over her stomach.

Another bolt of pain shot through her body, almost causing her to fall off her bed. Looking up again she saw Harold unconscious next to his bed and Sariana looking back at her, her eyes filled with agony. In the far corner of the room she saw Magnus sitting against the wall with his knees pulled to his chest. Through her cries she heard him moan.

Another spasm gripped her body. Her muscles tightened and her back arched as her vision blurred and she lost consciousness again.

***

Katalya opened her eyes as the pain that had consumed her for days had settled to a continuous deep ache, as if it came from her organs themselves.

She heard unfamiliar voices in the cell and looked toward Harold's bed. She saw two techs, escorted by a guard, carrying Harold from the room. As they moved, Harold's right arm fell limply to the floor.

"Only one of five," replied one of the techs. "Better than average."

"Still another phase and the final immunity check," said the other.

"Wh — what are you doing?" she huffed.

"Taking out the trash," replied the guard. "Unless you like sleeping with a corpse."

Katalya tried to push herself out of the bed but her muscles wouldn't respond; she could only watch as the two techs removed Harold's body. Once they left, two additional techs entered, each carrying a small satchel.

One of the techs walked over to her. Katalya wanted to turn away from him but didn't have the strength. She stared at him blankly as he took her hand and placed a medical scanner over her wrist. The scanner *beeped* and the tech moved the scanner from her wrist over her stomach and chest, eventually stopping on her forehead. As the scanner *beeped* again, the tech pulled a recording device from the satchel. "Subject 807 progressing to Phase Two," he spoke into the recorder. "Injecting final serum series."

Her eyes followed the injector until she lost sight of it, just before he drove it into her neck.

"Now the fun starts," he said with a dry smile as she felt the thick serum begin to move through her veins.

Suddenly, her head felt as if it was coming apart from the inside. She began to shake violently, saliva pouring from the side of her mouth.

She heard a scream from Dari just before she let out her own cry of agony.

Chapter 16

Katalya slowly swung her feet out of her bed. It had been two weeks since the first injection and three days since the second — all of which was a blur of pain and agony.

But today was different. Her body ached and her head felt like one large, raw nerve, but her body wanted to move. She needed to move.

Her feet touched the floor and the sensation raced through her body. Everything felt different.

Everything was different.

She had heard the hum of the ventilation in the room for weeks but today she heard the turning of each blade of the fan in duct. The details of the flooring, the walls — everything — it seemed like she had been looking at the world through a fog before. She saw a piece of lint drifting across the floor under the bed where

Harold had died. But she didn't just see it; Katalya saw the branches and contour of the miniscule ball of dirt as it bounced across the floor.

"Do you feel it?"

Katalya looked up to see Magnus standing at the edge of her bed. Even he looked different to her. He looked like … like someone she had known her whole life … almost as if he were family. "Yes."

"Close your eyes," he said.

She complied.

Her nose twitched and she began to see images of the room from the scent of the air.

She opened her eyes. "What is this?"

"Whatever they are wanting us to become," replied Magnus, "we will use as a weapon against them."

She could feel her heart pumping hard and strong with each beat. Despite the constant pain, she felt alive in a way she never had before. Everything was intensified. Her senses, the agony of loss she had experienced in her life … and the hatred for those that had caused her pain.

A bolt of pain shot throughout her jawline and she felt her hair straighten as she thought about Tamar, the man who had mercilessly abused her mother and who had led the raiders that destroyed her own family. With a groan, she looked up toward Magnus.

"Feel them."

Katalya moved her hand to her mouth and quickly pulled it away as she felt the hard, sharp outline of powerful canine teeth. "Like mother," she whispered.

"They come out when you're threatened or angry ... it feels —"

"Good," interrupted Katalya.

"Is everyone okay?" asked Sariana. "Do you feel —"

"Yes," said Dari, joining the group. "Are you —"

Dari was interrupted by Katalya's embrace.

Katalya wrapped her arms around Dari, squeezing her tightly. "You were always stronger than me," she said. "I would have let myself die if you hadn't been there for me." She looked into Dari's eyes as tears began to fall from hers. "Sister," she said quietly and rested her forehead against Dari's.

"What is next?" asked Sariana. "They must have done this for a reason."

"I do not know," replied Magnus. "But I can promise they will get much more than they expect."

***

The next morning Katalya awoke to the footsteps of people approaching her cell. Before the injections she wouldn't have heard them, but now ... they were still several meters away when she sat up in her bed.

Magnus was already up and standing near the door.

As she joined Magnus, Katalya could hear the men talking outside.

"Remember, just toss it in," said one of the men. "They're haven't had the control phase yet."

"Why don't they do that first?" asked the other man.

"Do I look like an Association scientist?" replied the first man. "It's gotta be something with the genetic sequencing," he added, "but I'm not paid to think about that."

"Be careful with that," warned the second man.

Katalya looked at Magnus. "What are they talking about?"

A small opening appeared above door and a canister fell at Katalya's feet.

"What is it?" she asked, backing away.

"I don't know," replied Magnus.

From several meters away, she could still see every detail of the canister. It was less than 10 centimeters long and two centimeters in diameter. All along the circumference were tiny holes. The canister was labeled. SERUM CONTAGION PHASE III.

"I don't like this," said Sariana.

"Maybe it's like the stuff they've been injecting into us," said Dari.

"Just stay away from it," warned Magnus. "This is different."

Well it doesn't really matter," replied Katalya. "It's not like we can do anything about it now." She stepped close to Magnus. "You need to get us ready to fight," she demanded. "No more waiting."

***

Katalya leapt in the air, wrapping her legs around Magnus' neck. She twisted her torso and sent the massive man tumbling to the ground.

He hit the floor and rolled back onto his knees as Katalya pounced again.

This time he caught her mid-air and drove her body onto the bed behind her. Quickly regaining her composure, she grabbed Magnus' right arm and swung her left leg against his neck, while shoving her right underneath his armpit. Pulling tightly, she heard him grunt.

"Okay, okay," he relented.

Katalya released her hold and jumped to her feet. "How did I do?"

"Good," replied Magnus, holding his elbow. "I thought you said you didn't know how to fight?"

"I don't," she replied.

"Then how where did you learn to move like that?"

"I don't know … it just seemed like the right thing to do … I didn't think about it; I just did it."

"And you two, as well," added Magnus, looking toward Dari and Sariana. "Regular people don't pick up fighting the way you have."

"I don't think we're regular anymore," replied Dari.

"The injections," declared Katalya.

"They have increased our speed and strength," said Magnus. "But it must have also improved our reflexes and our … I don't know … but you three are already as good at hand-to-hand as most soldiers from my home planet."

"I've never fought once in my life," said Sariana. "But …" She stopped to cough. "But I can just see in my mind what I'm supposed …" She coughed again. "… I'm supposed to do."

"You okay?" asked Dari.

"Yeah," replied Sariana. "I mean other than the aching muscles and headaches we've all had for weeks."

"You look a little pale," said Katalya.

"I'm fine," said Sariana. "Let's get back to it."

***

Katalya awoke to the sound of Sariana coughing and walked over to her bed.

"Sariana, are you okay?"

Sariana's complexion was pale and beads of sweat covered her face and arms. Her corneas were speckled with red as blood vessels began to rupture.

"Ha … hard to … br … breath," she coughed.

Katalya saw a small trickle of blood roll from the corner of Sariana's mouth.

"You're —"

"Dying," whispered Sariana. "I —" A series of powerful coughs prevented her from finishing.

"She's doesn't look good," said Dari as she joined Katalya. "I'll get her some water."

"It must be that canister," said Magnus.

"But why …" Sariana coughed and more blood pooled in her mouth. "… why would they make us sick?"

"Why would they turn us into … whatever we have become?" replied Katalya.

"Sariana!" yelled Dari as Sariana began to convulse. Blood and foam filled her mouth and her body shook.

Katalya held Sariana's clammy hand while her muscles spasmed. "No!" she whispered. "Not another one of us!"

Suddenly the convulsions stopped.

Katalya looked into Sariana's vacant eyes. Her struggle was over. Still holding Sariana's hand, she looked up toward Magnus. "Tomorrow," she said. "We fight back tomorrow."

"Tomorrow," replied Magnus.

***

Katalya felt the sharp canine teeth break through her skin as she stood ready for the guards to open the door. She glanced back toward Sariana's body. They would pay today.

Her senses were alert like never before as she heard shuffling outside of her cell. Her eyes were focused on the door and she could smell the guards on the other side of the wall. Her muscles twitched and her mouth began to salivate. She wanted to taste their blood.

Again the port above the door opened and another canister hit the ground.

This one looked different.

"Cover your —" Magnus' warning was drowned out by a loud explosion and a high-pitched piercing noise accompanied by a brilliant flash of light.

Katalya stumbled backward, blinded from the flash and disoriented from the piercing shrill of the grenade. A sting on her shoulder drew her attention just before a bolt of electricity ripped through her body and she lost consciousness.

Katalya shook her head as she slowly pushed herself off the floor. The smell of the guards was gone. She looked around the room to confirm it. "Wh ... what was that?"

"It was a flash grenade," answered Magnus, leaning against the wall of the cell.

Katalya felt a new ache in her forearm and looked down to see what appeared to be the circular outline of another injection. "Check your arms," she said, raising hers to the others.

"I've got one too," said Dari.

"They've injected us with something else," said Magnus, his face tight in a scowl.

"Does anyone feel anything?" asked Dari, almost frantic. "What's going to happen next ... I can't take much more of this," she added as she collapsed onto her bed.

"Nothing," replied Katalya. "Maybe it takes longer to —"

The door to the cell slid open and three guards stepped inside.

Katalya felt her muscles tighten and her canines extended further from her mouth. A guttural growl escaped her body. It was time to release her rage.

"Kneel!" came a voice from behind the guards.

Without realizing it, Katalya was on her knees. She tried to stand but a sharp pain raced down her spine. Panting as she struggled to regain control of her body, she looked up to see two Xen dressed in military uniform enter the cell.

She glanced toward Dari and then Magnus. They were on their knees.

"Looks like they're neutered," said one of the guards.

"It appears the control serum is effective on this batch," said one of the Xen.

"But not others," replied the other. "Still too many questions."

"These creatures' anatomies are complicated."

Katalya gritted her teeth and pushed herself to her feet.

The guards leveled their weapons on her. "Kneel!" shouted one of the Xen.

Pain tore through the back of her head and she fell to her knees again. Inhaling and exhaling heavily, Katalya's thoughts went to her mother. *'Was this what she was fighting when they killed her? If she could resist, so can I,'* she thought.

"Similar to the Vulpes strain, the Lupus had tendencies toward defiance," said one of the creatures.

"Perhaps the third strain will provide better results," replied the other.

Despite the pain, Katalya felt she could rise again. The thought of sinking her teeth into the brown, scaly creature caused saliva to pool in the corner of her mouth and her stomach tightened as if she hadn't eaten in days. She prepared to pounce but glanced toward Magnus. Surely the warrior would be able to resist better than her. Why hadn't he attacked?

Their gaze met. It was if he was speaking to her with his eyes. 'Why,' she screamed with her eyes, but remained on her knees. Her skin burned with rage as the Xen continued to talk.

"These will be able to continue," said one of the creatures to the guards.

Katalya's blood boiled as the Xen and the guards exited the cell. When the door shut, she exploded.

"Why the fuck didn't we kill them?" she shouted, storming toward Magnus, grabbing his shirt and shoving him.

"Calm down, Katalya," he pleaded. "There's a reason —"

"You preached resistance … you told me that if I didn't fight, I might as well be dead," she spat. "Well I'm ready and able to fight — all of us are. And now you say no."

She let out a gasp as Magnus picked her off the floor and pinned her against the wall. She struggled but he was too strong.

"Shut up and listen to me," he growled. He let out a heavy breath and lowered her to the floor. "You were able to resist, too," he said. "And you?" he asked turning toward Dari.

"Yes," said Dari. "I was waiting for you."

"Then we could have killed them all," growled Katalya.

"Then what?" asked Magnus.

"Then they would have been dead."

"And we would have done what ... wait for more guards."

"At least we would have taken a lot of them with us."

"Then we would have died like the animals they think we are," replied Magnus, placing his hand to Katalya's cheek. "We're more than that."

"Then what are we supposed to do?" huffed an exasperated Katalya.

"They think we are their pets," replied Magnus. "We can use that. They think we are compliant, so they will make mistakes ... let us see and hear things."

"What kind of things?" asked Dari.

"Everything," said Magnus. "We can see if others like us are ready to resist. We can learn about their strengths, their weaknesses ... this facility. Then we might be able to do more than just kill a few guards."

Chapter 17

Katalya walked down the passageway, a guard close behind. Four weeks had passed since Sariana died and the constant pain in Katalya's bones and muscles finally began to pass. All that remained was hatred. She could tell by the sound of his footsteps he had an old injury to his left leg and could smell that he had had beef for his last meal. He had no idea how easy it would be for her to tear his throat out.

But Magnus had been right. Believing Katalya and others were under their control, the Xen began to use them for manual labor in addition to the almost daily battery of testing. The labor had allowed them, often under the watch of a single guard, to move about the facility. After the first week, they were paired with other groups to clear foliage on the facility perimeter. And they had shared their stories. In a short period of time, they had learned so much about both the Xen and the other captives.

Turning the corner, her attention was drawn to a row of new captives being shuffled toward her. Her thoughts flashed to day she arrived. So much had changed.

One of the captives looked up toward her, her eyes full of fear and anxiety. Katalya smiled back at her. "Fight," she mouthed.

So much had changed indeed.

"Keep moving!" The familiar voice exploded in her consciousness, her canines deployed, and her skin grew hot as she looked up to see Tamar prodding the new batch of captives. Tamar saw her and smiled. "I know you," he smiled. "You're the biter."

"We're all biters now," she replied, allowing her canines to show.

"Keep your dog in line," said Tamar to Katalya's guard as he gripped his rifle. "Or I'll do it for you."

"Move!" ordered Katalya's guard.

The shot of pain accompanied with each order ran down her spine, but she knew it wouldn't stop her from killing her guard and ripping out Tamar's jugular.

But Magnus was right, so she turned away from Tamar and continued walking.

A few meters down the hallway another captive and guard approached. It was a woman in her late teens with blonde hair and blue eyes. As soon as she made eye contact with the other captive, her instinctive defenses heightened. Every muscle in her body urged her to attack the stranger approaching her. The woman's scent … it smelled like … an enemy.

Katalya felt her larynx vibrating in a low growl.

The other woman let out an audible grunt and lunged toward Katalya.

Katalya tensed, ready to receive her attacker.

"Stop!" shouted the woman's guard and Katalya's attacker instantly stopped but stood tense, fangs protruding from her mouth.

"Damn it!" cursed Katalya's guard. "What the fuck are you doing here?"

"Taking this one to the test chamber on Level 2 of B wing," replied the guard.

"You're on the wrong fucking level," cursed Katalya's guard. "You're supposed to keep the Serum 3 ones away from the others. They don't play well with each other."

"Sorry, man. But these ones aren't any trouble at all. Literally like trained dogs."

Katalya's guard laughed. "Well that's a nice-looking dog you got there."

"Yours too," replied the other guard, looking over Katalya's body. "But I don't want anything to do with those wolf-bitches … too unpredictable. I'd rather not have my hand … or anything else … bit off."

"They're a bit of trouble but we just put down the ones that don't listen."

"All of these ones listen," said the other guard. "It almost seems like following orders makes them happy."

"Well I guess that's why the rest are being discontinued," said Katalya's guard. "I —" The guard paused when Katalya turned toward him.

She could tell he knew he had said too much.

"Well you better get that one back to the right level," said Katalya's guard.

***

Katalya's head ached as she contemplated the work 'discontinued' on her walk back to her cell. And what made her hate the other captive so much?

"In," directed the guard as he opened the door.

Katalya stepped inside to see Dari sitting in the center of the cell. Her head was facing the floor and her shoulders hunched forward. Her blonde hair was stained with splotches of blood — blood that smelled similar to the woman Katalya had met in the passageway.

"Are you okay?"

Dari looked up toward Katalya. Tears streamed down her face — a face soaked in blood.

"Dari?"

"I killed him," she sobbed. "And I enjoyed it."

"What?"

"It was a man ... a boy. Maybe eighteen."

"Where?" asked Katalya. "What are you talking about?"

"In the test room. They put me in the empty room and then sent him in ..." She paused, taking in a deep breath. "While those things just watched from above."

Katalya placed her hand on Katalya's shoulder, she knew what had happened.

"I saw him and I ... I —"

"Hated him," interrupted Katalya.

"Yes," huffed Dari. "Then they ordered us to fight ... but I resisted."

"And he didn't."

"No. He charged me and I had to defend myself. Once we started fighting, I stopped thinking." She took another heavy breath. "When I bit him ... I just ... it was like nothing else mattered but killing him."

"They've made us that way," said Katalya. "And it kept you alive."

"I hate them," cried Dari. "All of them."

"Their time will come," said Katalya. "And it will come soon; it has too. Magnus should be back from his work detail soon and we will talk to him."

***

Katalya, Dari, and Magnus sat in the center of their cell.

"He said discontinue?" asked Magnus.

"What does that mean?" asked Dari, still running her hands through her wet hair, checking for blood that was no longer there.

"Nothing good," replied Katalya. "And those other captives…"

"They are a new strain," said Magnus. "I was able to talk with Horatio from A4. Apparently, the Xen have been testing the wolf and fox strains for several years. The fox —"

"Like my mother," interrupted Katalya.

"Yes. The fox proved resistant … as have most of the wolf." He paused. "Even with the ones like us playing along, they still weren't satisfied so they began testing with a third serum. It looks like these new ones have been mixed with Humani war dog DNA. They are … different than us."

"How?" asked Katalya. "I know when I saw the one … it was all I could do not to attack."

"I'm pretty sure a wolf and a Humani war dog would be natural enemies," said Magnus.

"But what is more important is the new ones seem to be not only completely obedient but fiercely loyal to their masters."

"Discontinued," said Katalya, realizing their fate. "They don't need us anymore."

"They're going to kill us all," said Dari.

"Is it time now?" asked Katalya.

"It is," replied Magnus. "I'll get word to Horatio and the one they call Elder tomorrow."

Later that night Katalya stared at the ceiling of her cell, unable to sleep. She heard Magnus approach her bed.

"Can't sleep?"

"No," she replied, sitting up in her bed. "I've just been thinking about … everything."

He sat beside her and placed his hand on hers.

"I know you have been frustrated with me, but I just wanted to give us the best chance to actually escape. To survive."

"Do you think we'll escape?"

"I don't know. Even if we …" He paused. "I don't know."

"Either way," she said, scooting closer to him. The pressure of his leg against hers made her stomach tighten and her pulse quicken. "I would have given up long ago if not for you and Dari," she added with a glance toward her sleeping friend. "There has just been so much pain. My parents, then my family … Sierra is …

I don't know …" A tear fell down her cheek. "I think about what could be happening to her and …" She took a deep breath. "Sometimes I hope she is dead." More tears fell as she looked into Magnus' eyes. "What does that make me?" she pleaded.

"I could tell you had been hurt," he said. "But I think it makes you someone who loves their family." Magnus caressed her cheek and looked into her eyes.

"But since the change," she continued, "I just want to protect my brothers and sisters … and kill these animals holding us here. Maybe then, someday, I will find my Sierra."

"When the time comes, you will get vengeance and I will help you when you are ready to find your girl, but …" He placed his other hand on her opposite cheek. "I don't want you take any chances that will prevent you from escaping." His eyes looked into her soul as he continued. "I don't want to lose you."

"You won't," she replied, leaning in to kiss him.

Chapter 18

Katalya was startled from her sleep by the sound of footsteps rushing toward the cell. Before she could react, the door opened. Rising to her feet, she was joined by Magnus and Dari as four guards entered the room.

"Get in line!" ordered one of the guards.

Something was wrong but Katalya knew they would have to play along. A glance toward Magnus returned a nod and she joined him and Dari in line.

"Move."

The three made their way down the passageway similar to many other trips. At the second corridor, however, the lead guard turned right instead of left. She looked back toward Magnus.

"Keep moving," ordered one of the guards from behind the group.

As they continued, her nose caught a familiar scent. Looking forward she saw another group join them from an adjoining passageway. It was Horatio and others from the same serum group, including his mate, Kendra. They all exchanged glances as the two groups were herded together and continued down the corridor. Now eight strong and surrounded by ten guards, they continued to move down the passageway. Every few meters, the passageway grew wider and more joined them. In a short period of time, hundreds of captives were being pushed through the corridor.

"This is it," whispered Magnus. "Today we will fight or die."

"When?" asked Katalya, her pulse quickening.

"When Elder acts," he replied with a glance to a man a few meters in front of them. He was as tall as Magnus and perhaps even broader. Elder's head and shoulders stood out above the crowd. His salt-and-pepper hair was cut short, accentuating the pointed edges of his ears and his elongated jawline. He glanced back toward Magnus, who gave a nod of subservience.

She had never seen Magnus defer to anyone.

"Who is he?" she asked although she could almost smell his dominance.

"Our leader," he replied. "He has organized many other small groups just like ours."

"Stop!" shouted a guard at the head of the group.

Katalya's attention was drawn to a long series of doors on the wall in front of the group.

"This is where they're going to kill us," said Dari.

"Move!" another guard yelled from the front.

Katalya's sensitive ears picked up murmuring and the rapid shuffling of feet from the van of the group. The restlessness was almost electric; Katalya's fangs extended and her hair bristled.

"I said move!" came an unsettled order from another guard.

A guard a few feet from Katalya shoved another captive. The captive, a woman with thick black hair, regained her footing and stared defiantly at the guard.

Suddenly a howl rolled over the crowed.

Katalya's heart pumped hard as she saw the man called Elder raising his head into the air.

Another joined in.

Soon low, guttural growls echoed off the walls and Katalya felt like her heart would explode from her chest.

"Everyone on your knees!" shouted a guard from a platform above them with his rifle leveled toward the crowed.

The pain in the base of her skull felt like a small itch compared to the rage and excitement racing through her body.

"Now!" shouted Elder.

Katalya's vision tunneled on a guard a few feet away and she lunged toward him. The large corridor exploded with growls and gunfire.

The guard, his senses overwhelmed by the chaos, saw Katalya too late. She crashed into him, her teeth sinking into his neck. The salty taste and the warm flow of blood over her mouth sent a bolt of excitement through her body. She twisted her head violently and the guard let out a terrified scream. Looking down at her victim as blood poured from his neck, she could see the terror in his eyes. She pulled a knife from the guard's vest and drove it into his temple, letting out a grunt as she did.

Grabbing the guard's rifle, she sensed movement and turned to see a rifled leveled at her head. Before she could react, Magnus' large hand palmed the guard's head and in a powerful motion sent him flying. The guard hit the ground and attempted to turn his rifle on Magnus, but it was too late. Both Magnus and Katalya's weapons erupted as the crackling of gunfire and the symphony of growls and screams were soon joined by the blaring of alarms.

"Come! We follow Elder," he panted as he pulled Katalya to her feet, his mouth soaked in the blood of one of his captors.

She looked to see Elder leading a group of about fifteen away from the series of doors.

"Let's go!" shouted Magnus and the two raced toward their leader.

Rushing toward Elder, she saw Magnus shift his rifle from his left to right and back, firing at targets as they ran. She had forgotten he had been some kind of soldier before the change.

In a few seconds, they joined Elder and the others at the corner leading to the next passageway.

Katalya looked back toward the double doors behind the hundreds of captives and guards locked in combat. It was a bloody ballet of death and guards and captives fought for their lives.

Suddenly the chaotic noise was drowned out by the deafening thud of heavy automatic weapons.

Katalya gasped as she saw dozens mowed down, the lead cutting large swaths through guard and captive alike. "They're killing their own men," she declared.

"The Xen don't care about the guards any more than us," replied Elder. He turned toward Magnus. "We need to get back to the housing wing. From there we can try to make it to the perimeter and the forest."

Even with the turmoil going on around her, Katalya was mesmerized by Elder's eyes. They at the same time radiated ferocity and a confident calm. No wonder Magnus followed to him.

"Magnus. You and Kal take the point and move forward." He turned toward Horatio. "Horatio. You cover our retreat. Everyone else stay in line and move quickly. If you have a rifle and know how to use them, follow the lead of Magnus and Horatio."

"What if we don't have a weapon?" asked Dari.

Elder placed his hand on Dari's shoulder, letting his fangs show. "We all have weapons, sister." He turned back toward Magnus. "Let's go."

"Yes, Elder," replied Magnus before moving forward.

***

The group of twenty rushed down the passageways of the facility. Echoes of gunfire and explosions mixed with muffled screams rang in Katalya's ears. Staying close to Magnus, she was in the front of the pack as the group made the last turn toward their cells.

She dropped to her knees when she saw Magnus curl backwards toward the ground. Looking down the barrel of her rifle, she saw four Xen soldiers. Her sights aligned on the torso of one and she fired. The sound of Mangus' and Kal's rifles joined hers as she saw a flash of brown and green.

She turned to see Kal throw a Xen soldier to the ground. Before the creature could move, Kal peppered his body with bullets from his rifle.

"The fucking thing bit me," cursed the former smuggler, blood beginning to soak through the front of his shirt just below his collarbone.

"Are you okay, brother?" asked Magnus, glancing toward Kal as he kept his rifle forward.

"I'm fine," replied Kal. "I —," He coughed. Then staggered.

Kal pulled the collar of his shirt down to look at his wound. Katalya could see the skin on his collarbone blackening, with dark trails of poison crawling up his neck underneath his skin.

"I —" Kal fell to the ground and began to convulse.

"Don't let them bite you," Elder warned Katalya as he knelt beside Kal. "Their bite is deadly ..." He looked down toward Kal, who was already gasping for air. "And quick."

"We have to keep moving," said Magnus.

"We can't leave Ka —"

"He's already dead," interrupted Elder. "Magnus is right."

With one quick glance toward Kal's frozen eyes, Katalya joined the others as they ran toward their cells.

They passed their cells and moved toward the staging areas for the work teams. Leaving the housing area, the group slowly moved into laboratory areas. Katalya knelt next to Magnus as they took cover outside one of the labs in a corridor leading to a maintenance room.

"Once we get through here," said Elder, "we'll move through corridor 7F and then —"

An explosion jarred Katalya, almost knocking her unconscious. As debris floated to the ground around her, Katalya looked back to the squad of Xen soldiers rushing them.

The group collided in an explosion of growls, hisses, and teeth.

Katalya grabbed the torso of a Xen soldier and rolled on top of him. As the creature snapped at her with its long snout, she pressed its head to one side and sank her teeth into its neck with a growl.

The Xen's blood tasted sweet, almost like candy, as she bit down hard. She sensed her jaws come together and pulled away with a mouthful of the Xen's neck.

Just as she was ready to bite down again, a burst of gunfire sent a volley of bullets into the wall just above her head. Instinctively, she rolled away and into the lab.

Inside the lab Katalya jumped to her feet and looked around the room. She didn't see anyone. But she could smell them. The scent made her skin grow hot and her heart quicken with anger. Closing her eyes, she took in a deep breath.

She knew where he was.

Katalya walked over to a large storage locker and with her rifle at the ready, swung the door open. Inside, hunkered in the corner, was Tamar with his pistol pointed toward her.

She flinched as he pulled the trigger.

Click. It was empty.

She raised her rifle, pressing it to his forehead.

But she didn't pull the trigger. She stared into his eyes as her mind was flooded with images of her mother … her husband … her children. The fight for survival between the Xen and her companions going on only meters away faded from her consciousness as the need for revenge consumed her. She lowered her rifle and stepped backwards.

Tamar slowly stood. "I know you," he said, drawing a knife from his vest. "The biter ... You and that other little bitch killed one of my boys."

"You knew my mother, too," she replied, her mouth wet with saliva.

"I'm afraid I don't remember." Tamar stepped from the closet as he presented a second knife. "I've known a lot of mothers in my time, girl," he replied with a smile. "And sisters ... and daughters and —"

"Well you will remember them because I whisper their names in your ear as you die."

"And you're not the first person to threaten me eith —"

Katalya was on him.

A glancing blow from one of his blades sliced into her hip but she didn't feel it as she drove him against the wall. Twisting one arm downward violently, she heard his elbow snap just before she sank her teeth into his other forearm.

Tamar dropped both of his blades and let out a groan that transitioned to a cry of agony as she shifted her stance and sank her teeth into the side of his face. Pulling away, she saw the white of his jawbone as she spat the meat from her mouth.

"Do you remember?" she growled.

He looked up, his eyes wide from pain and fear as blood oozed from the gruesome gash in his cheek.

She opened her mouth wide and with all of her rage drove her fangs into his neck. She ripped away the flesh and bit down again. Blood sprayed over her face and torso.

With blood coating her body, she leaned in close to Tamar's ear. "This is for all of them — every mother, daughter, and sister ..." Tears rolled down her cheeks, mixing with the blood that was now thick on her skin. "But the last thing you will hear," she added, looking up to see the light begin to fade from his eyes, "... Sierra."

With another growl she sank her teeth into his neck again, holding her grip until she felt the last beat of his heart.

"Katalya!" shouted Magnus, bursting into the room.

He froze when he saw her blood-soaked face as she knelt over Tamar's body.

"He ... my mother," she said as she stood, her fangs still dripping Tamar's lifeblood.

"Good," he replied, placing his hand on the back of her head. "We must go."

Exiting the lab, she looked over the carnage in the passageway. Bodies of Xen and captives were strewn everywhere and the floor was slick with greenish-blue and red blood.

"Quickly," directed Elder. "The exit is nearby."

"What happened?" asked Dari, seeing the blood covering Katalya.

"The one who took us … who killed Charles and …" She took a deep breath.

"He's dead?"

Katalya nodded.

"Good," she replied. "I told you your time for revenge would —"

Dari fell backwards as gunfire again erupted.

"Dari!" yelled Katalya, falling to the ground with Dari. Katalya ran her hands over Dari's body, looking for injuries. Her hands stopped over her stomach as she felt the warmth of Dari's blood. She looked down to the see blood quickly soaking through her shirt. "Dari … you're … someone give me a medical pack!"

"We're out," declared Magnus as he dug through his pack. He scanned the bodies of the Xen. "There's none here."

"It'll be okay," huffed Dari. "I can … get … up," she stammered as she tried to push herself off the floor only to fall onto her back again.

"I'll carry you," said Katalya. "I'm not leaving you."

Another burst of gunfire from behind them was answered by a salvo from the captives with rifles.

"There's more of them coming," reported one of the captives. "We have to go."

Katalya slid her hand under Dari's torso.

"No," replied Dari pushing Katalya away. "I'm not going to slow you down."

"I'm not leaving —"

"You are," interrupted Dari. "I'm going to die," she continued, placing her hand against Katalya's cheek. "And you know it — we don't have any meds and if I slow the group down …"

"But I can't leave you," huffed Katalya. "I —"

"I will die free and if you live, then I will live in your heart."

Magnus fired another burst from his rifle. "We have to go!" he shouted, reaching down to grab Dari.

"Stop!" she growled as blood pooled around her lips. "I'll make sure they don't follow."

"No!" cried Katalya.

"Take her!" ordered Dari, grimacing.

Magnus looked toward Elder.

The leader nodded.

"You will not be forgotten," said Magnus as she stood, grabbing Katalya's arm.

Katalya broke away from Magnus' grip and fell to her knees beside Dari. "You are truly my sister," she sobbed.

Dari smiled. "Now go," she replied with a glance toward Magnus.

Katalya felt Magnus grab her again, pulling her to feet. She struggled at first but conceded as Magnus drug her away from Dari and toward the exit.

***

"Slow!" shouted a senior guard who moved forward through the human wreckage of the passageway. He glanced back toward the five men behind him. "Check the side doors but be quick … they're probably headed for the exit."

He scanned the floor.

"Movement!" he shouted as he stepped toward the body of a woman.

He pressed the barrel of his rifle against her shoulder and rolled her onto her back. As she rolled over, he saw her torso soaked in blood and an old scar on her face. She was breathing heavily, almost panting as death began to take her.

"Should've just went along," said the guard. "It would have been quicker … but you reap what you sow."

Her eyes slowly focused on him.

"Any last words?" he said with a smile as she raised his rifle to his shoulder.

The woman's eyes opened wide and fangs flashed bright. "Die!" she growled as she pulled the man to the ground, spinning him around and sinking her teeth into his neck.

The other guards leveled their weapons.

Her teeth still embedded in the guard's neck, Dari pulled the pin from one of the grenades on the guard's vest as the guards opened fire.

***

"Once the doors open, head south to the perimeter fence," said Elder. "If we can make it the first few hundred meters, the vegetation gets dense."

"After that?" asked a captive.

"We stay together until we find a good place for cover," replied Magnus.

The crackling of gunfire followed by the roar of an explosion rattled the floor underneath Katalya's feet, causing her to look down the passageway. She looked back toward Magnus.

"She died for all of us," he replied.

The facility door slid open.

"Move!" shouted Elder.

Chapter 19

Katalya let out a deep breath as the Xen patrol faded into the thick forest. She slowly lowered the cover to the entrance of the tunnel. "That was close," she whispered to Magnus.

"But a good sign," replied Magnus. "The number of patrols is down. I think they either think they've killed all of us or maybe they have just given up."

"They have killed most of us," sighed Katalya.

"But not all of us," he replied, pressing his hand to her cheek. "And if one of us lives ... all of us do."

"Let's get back to the clan," she said with a forced smile.

***

Katalya sat beside Magnus in a makeshift hall deep underneath the surface of Navato as the Elder addressed the clan. Magnus placed his hand on her thigh and she glanced at him, smiling.

"We may have been lucky to find these caves and that the Xen were not aware of them," said Elder. "But our resolve and unity have allowed us to thrive over the last months. They sent patrols after us — we either evaded or killed them. Then they sent their mutts after us …"

Katalya felt her teeth moving at the mention of the fanatical canine slaves that replaced the wolf and fox clans as Xen test subjects.

"We lost many in the first few weeks, but we killed so many of their pets that they stopped sending them," he continued, his eyes almost glowing. "And just as the wolf adapts, so have we. We may be living in darkness, but we are living by the rule of the pack and not the lizards."

Katalya felt Magnus give her thigh a squeeze. She knew he almost worshipped Elder, but so did everyone else. It seemed the combination of his leadership and the genetic alterations of the Xen testing had created an almost unavoidable compulsion to follow the ones best suited by strength and intelligence to lead.

"And we will continue to adapt and thrive," said Elder. "I have called this meeting to share great news for the clan." He looked toward Horatio and Kendra. "Brother Horatio ... sister Kendra, stand," he ordered.

The two stood.

"They will be the first to bring new life into our clan," he said with a smile.

The room erupted with cheers and howls of happiness.

"We are blessed and proud to bring more strength to the clan," said Horatio. "And thanks to sister Yayla and her medical knowledge, we know we will have a daughter."

More cheers and howls filled the room.

"We will raise her to be strong of heart, fierce in the fight, and to follow the pack regardless of the cost," continued Horatio.

"We will call her Dari," added Kendra with a glance toward Katalya.

Epilogue

Two years later ...

Astra Varus let out a frustrated breath as she tugged at her father's shoulder. "Why are we here, father?" she pouted. "It's bad enough you are making me marry that ... that commoner."

"You know he is not a commoner," replied Senator Dominotra Varus. "Major Stone is a member of the Lucius family, which you know has been very helpful to us with recent political activities. And, once the engagement is solidified, they will restore his name." He placed his hand on hers. "It is a good marriage," he said with a smile. "His family's military record will be just what we need for expanding the influence of our family ... and yours."

"I guess," huffed Astra. "But why did you drag me off to this horrible place?"

"Few know of what I am about to show you," replied Dominotra. "That is why we have to travel to Capro. The majority of the Senate think all of Capro's facilities are for prisoners, but this facility is different."

"How?" demanded Astra. "Just show me so we can get off of this rock."

"There," replied Dominotra, "through the window."

Astra looked at the obstacle course set up on the opposite side of the viewing window.

As she looked on, a group of ten young adults walked onto the course through a set of large metal doors.

"We're going to watch people playing?" she huffed.

"Watch," he replied.

A bell rang and the group burst into a sprint. Astra's jaw gaped as she realized the speed at which they were moving. In the lead was a woman with her jet-black hair, cut short to her shoulders. Leaping over an obstacle, the woman jumped almost three meters onto a climbing wall before grabbing the rope. Taking the rope in her hands, she pulled her body upward and kicked her torso over the top of the obstacle. Jumping to the ground on the opposite side, she took two long strides and leapt over a three-meter water obstacle. Hitting the ground again, she shoved a heavy block out of the way before sprinting across a thin beam without any concern for losing her balance. Crossing the beam, she grabbed a rifle and fired several rounds into three target drones, destroying each one.

Ejecting the magazine, she placed the rifle on the platform from which she grabbed it and came to attention.

"What am I watching?" asked Varus.

"You know the Directive and our plans with the Association?"

"Of course," replied Varus, "but …" She paused. "Are these ones altered?"

"Yes, Astra. But these are ours."

"Ours?"

Dominotra pressed a button on the wall next to the window. "Bring the leader up with one of the others," he said before turning back to Astra. "I made a deal with the Association to filter some of the younger ones out and send them here to Capro for independent testing. These were taken in adolescence, but it appears that after the young ones are altered, they experience rapid physical development during puberty, which also comes at a younger age compared to normal humanoids." He paused. "How old to you think they are?"

"I don't know, father … nineteen … twenty."

"The girl that finished first is no more than twelve."

"Twelve?" gasped Astra.

"Yes," smiled Dominotra. "And completely loyal to the First Families."

"Like a war dog?" asked Astra, a smile coming to her face.

The door slid open and a tall, black-haired woman walked into the room, a rifle slid over her shoulder. Behind her was a large, muscular male — also armed.

"The guns, father," said Astra, stepping backwards.

"Nothing to worry about," laughed Dominotra as he walked over to the woman.

"What is your directive, solider?" he asked.

"To follow the will of the First Families, kill all enemies of the Republic, and defend the Varus family to the death," replied the woman, bowing her head slightly to Dominotra.

A smile came to Astra's face. "Fascinating."

"That's not all," added Dominotra, with a smile. "Is that a knife in your vest?" he asked to woman.

"Yes, Master Varus."

"Very nice," he replied. "Now take that knife and kill your companion," he ordered.

In a flash, the woman snatched the blade from her vest and drove it into the neck of the large man, driving him into the ground. As they hit the ground, the woman twisted and jerked the blade from the man's neck, causing blood to spray almost a meter from the floor.

"Shit!" declared Astra, momentarily losing her composure.

The woman slowly rose to her feet, sliding the bloody knife back into its sheath as she stood over the body of her companion. "Are you pleased, Master Varus?"

"Very much," replied Dominotra, turning toward Astra.

"What is your name?" asked Astra.

"My name is Sierra, Mistress Varus," replied Katalya's daughter.

About the Author

Brian Dorsey is a retired Naval Officer and is currently a Nuclear Test Engineer for a Naval Shipyard. When not spending time with his family, Brian enjoys reading and researching US and Native American history, watching good TV shows or films (anything by Joss Whedon), hunting, teaching the occasional history class, or working on his next writing project.

Current books available in the Gateway Universe

Gateway (Gateway Series Book 1)
Cold Planet (A Gateway Universe Story)
Saint (Gateway Series Book 2)
Uprising (Gateway Series Book 3)
Rise of the Wolf: Katalya's Story (A Novella)
Schism (Gateway Series 4)

www.ingramcontent.com/pod-product-compliance
Lightning Source LLC
Chambersburg PA
CBHW030743110726
47900CB00008B/2424